The Art
of Argument

The Art
of Argument

Carlos Leroy Hunsinger

shley Books, Inc.
Port Washington, N. Y. 11050

THE ART OF ARGUMENT
© Copyright 1980, by Carlos Leroy Hunsinger.

Library of Congress Number: 79-15660
ISBN: 0-87949-163-9

ASHLEY BOOKS, INC./*Publishers*
Port Washington, New York 11050

Printed in the United States of America
First Edition

9 8 7 6 5 4 3 2 1

Library of Congress Cataloging in Publication Data:

HUNSINGER, CARLOS LEROY   1909 –
    The art of argument.

    1. Debates and debating. I. Title.
PN4181.H8   808.53   79-15660
ISBN 0-87949-163-9

Contents

The Art
of Argument

Introduction

Do you habitually think of the right answer *after* the argument is over? That is because you have not become sufficiently adept at the science of argument to be able to respond automatically with the right reply. For some people, the ability to come back with the correct retort is natural, but for others it must be learned by painstaking study and practice. This book is for this latter group.

I have come to the preparation of this work from a background of rich experience. Beginning when I first began to talk and continuing through the intervening forty-seven years, I have advanced by easy stages through the principles of beginning, intermediate, and advanced argumentative practice. During that time, I have confronted every type of argument, insinuation, and conversational trick known in the field of expert argumentation. The knowledge gained from these experiences, together with some trial-and-error innovations of my own, have given me sufficient background and insight to present some useful information to those who are still novices in the art of argument.

Indeed, these experiences have so impressed me with the magic of words in the field of controversy, and have given me such an ability to see and present each and every side of every question, that my wife, herself adept at the use of the subtle insinuations which can discredit the arguments of an opponent, has accused me of remaining silent on every question until some other person has expressed an opinion concerning it, and then taking issue on the opposite side.

This book is not presented as a treatise on logic, nor as a guide to winning friends and influencing people. The theme of this book, by contrast, might better be described as the presentation of techniques calculated to lose friends and obscure the truth in the overriding objective of winning arguments.

I do not claim that a person, following the principles laid down in this book, will be able in every case to convince other persons of the soundness of his point of view. I have found that other people, once they have expressed an opinion on any subject, are strangely impervious to arguments of any kind.

It is true that the use of these techniques may sometimes persuade persons other than the one with whom you are in direct argument. It is hoped, also, as an extra bonus, that experience with these techniques will foster an ability to recognize the many types of spurious arguments which beset us on every side, and which one should be on guard against in an earnest search for the truth. However, these are merely happy byproducts of the argumentative contest. The satisfaction of winning is still the main objective, and the person who will diligently follow the teachings in this book may always claim at least the semblance of victory over debating adversaries and will have the satisfaction of knowing that he will *never* have to admit that he was wrong.

1
Preparation for the Life of a Professional Argufier

To become really expert in the art of argument, you should give some thought to the kind of person you should become and the preparation you will need. There is the question, for example, of the amount of background preparation you should have in the subjects to be argued about. There are many who hold that you should be well grounded in the facts relating to those subjects in order to properly support your arguments.

However, I do not recommend this practice. The only effect of knowing all of the facts relating to a question is to *lessen* your assurance in discussing it, thus making your argument less effective. You should strive for the Biblical objective of being able to "speak as one having authority," which cannot be accomplished if you have any doubts about the rightness of your position as a result of having read or heard the facts supporting the other side. The only reason for ever studying the facts on the opposing side of a question is to be able to anticipate the opponent's arguments and to raise arguments to refute them. When this is the purpose of research on a subject it may be justified, but be sure in that case that you are not swayed by the opposing arguments.

Of even more importance is the maintenance of a stance of rightness which will make you seem more credible than your opponents to those who may hear or read their arguments. One of the most effective ways of doing this is to maintain an appearance of down-to-earth simplicity in approaching the questions under debate, and to present your opponents, in contrast, as skilled, clever arguers. This not only helps you to identify with the audience, but also helps to weaken and cast suspicion upon the sincerity and reasonableness of your opponents. This is a technique which was used effectively by Will Rogers in his famous preface, "Well, all I know is what I read in the newspapers."

In similar vein, Shakespeare has Mark Antony say in his famous burial oration for Caesar:

> I come not, friends, to steal away your hearts:
> I am no orator as Brutus is;
> But, as you know me all, a plain blunt man.

Lincoln was similarly adept at winning the confidence of his audience through his protestations of a lack of debating skill. In one of his early political speeches he said:

Fellow citizens of the state of Ohio: I cannot fail to remember that I appear for the first time before an audience... that is accustomed to hear such speakers as Corwin, and Chase, and Wade, and many other renowned men; and remembering this, I feel that it will be well for you and for me, that you should not raise your expectations to that standard to which you would have been justified in raising them had one of these distinguished men appeared before you.

On another occasion, Lincoln used the same technique, in reverse, to discredit a rival politician at the same time that he presented himself as a true man of the people. This rival politician, Colonel Dick Taylor, had been posing as a plain, simple man, while denouncing Lincoln and his group as "rag-barons and manufacturing lords." On one occasion, while Colonel Taylor was speaking, Lincoln rushed up on the platform and opened the Colonel's vest to disclose a ruffled shirt, gold watch and chain, seals and glittering jewels. Lincoln, in contrast, was attired in rough frontier dress. His remarks to the audience were devastating:

"Behold the hard-fisted Democrat!" he said. "Look, gentlemen, at this specimen of bone and sinew." Then, bowing to indicate his own homely person, he said, "And here, gentlemen here at your service, here is your *aristocrat*! Here is one of your silk-stockinged gentry. Here is your rag-baron with his lily-white hands. Yes, I suppose I, according to my friend Taylor, am a bloated aristocrat.

"While Colonel Taylor was making the charges against the Whigs all over the country," he continued, "riding in fine carriages, wearing ruffled shirts, kid gloves, massive gold watch-chains with large gold seals, and flourishing a gold-headed cane, I was a poor boy, hired on a flat-boat at eight dollars a month, and had only one pair of breeches to my back, and they buckskin. Now, if you know the nature of buckskin, when wet and dried by the sun it will shrink, and my breeches kept shrinking until they left several inches of my legs bare, between the tops of my socks and the lower part of my breeches; and while I was growing taller they were becoming shorter, and so much tighter that they left a blue streak around my legs that can be seen to this day. If you call this aristocracy, I plead guilty to the charge."

Socrates, too, used this technique (unsuccessfully, as it turned out) in his defense against the charges of irreverence and the corruption of Athenian youth. In this defense, as recorded in *The Apology*, he said:

> How you, O Athenians, have been affected by my accusers I cannot tell; but I know they almost made me forget who I was—so persuasively did they speak; and yet they have hardly uttered a

word of truth. But of the many falsehoods told by them, there was one which quite amazed me;—I mean when they said that you should be upon your guard and not allow yourself to be deceived by my force of eloquence. To say this when they were certain to be detected as soon as I opened my lips and proved myself to be anything but a great speaker, did indeed appear to me most shameless—unless by the force of eloquence they mean the force of truth; for if such is their meaning, I admit I am eloquent.

To make this technique really effective, you should build up a reputation as a person of practical common sense. You can do this by telling your listeners that you want to "talk sense" to them, thus implying that those who are arguing on the other side of the question have not been talking sense! You should also repeat in your arguments a statement that people should think for themselves, or that children should be taught to think for themselves. This is especially effective if your argument is based on an appeal to prejudice. For example, in advocating the teaching of patriotism in our schools, you should list the ability *to think* among the things this training should include.

Similarly, you should make a point of urging everyone to vote. "Vote for the candidate of your choice, but vote." No one will believe you really mean it, but it will make you seem like a reasonable, tolerant person.

Another effective means of building up a reputation for reasonableness is to adopt a practice of speaking often and vigorously on the popular side of every noncontroversial subject. Don't wait until you have a subject that you feel strongly about, because building up your reputation is something to be accomplished as soon as possible. Besides, any question which you feel strongly about will probably be controversial, and you cannot build a reputation for common-sense reasonableness if you devote time to ideas with which others might not agree. In fact, if you *must* disagree with popular opinion, you should limit those disagreements to instances in which you do feel strongly about a subject. Otherwise, you should go along with the majority. Make a point of expressing yourself as being opposed to such things as air pollution, drug abuse, and race discrimination, and in favor of such things as welfare reform, low-cost housing, and the elimination of poverty. If you are associated with a group which is unanimous in its opinion on some other subject, you may also express your agreement with that opinion when talking to members of that group. Then, if you should at some time find yourself involved in an argument on a controversial subject, your reputation for simple reasonableness will give you the benefit of the doubt, and help to convince your audience of the rightness of your argument.

Moreover, even though you might find yourself engaged in an unpopular argument, you can usually still maintain your reputation for reasonableness by presenting your argument in such a way as to make your motives appear to be worthy. For example, you may be in an argument over which of two proposed routes would be better for a highway which is planned for your area. You could have various reasons for favoring the route which you advocate, such as having a business alongside this propsed route which would be benefited by the increased traffic in that area, or a piece of property along the course of that route which you could sell to the government at a profit for the right of way, or perhaps a piece of property along the course of the other route which you would not wish to sell for the right of way. *You should never admit to any such reasons,* however, but should find some reason which would relate to the public good. Fortunately, whenever there is a controversy over two alternate highway routes, one of them is usually favored because it would be cheaper, while the other is favored because it would better serve the area, and you can latch onto whichever of these reasons would apply to the route you favor.

Similar considerations could apply to the question of demonstrations on college campuses. You might favor such demonstrations as a means of spreading political dissent and building up your own political following. Of course, you cannot announce or admit to these long-range goals of changing society, but must relate the demonstrations to some popular causes affecting education, such as the demand for a larger enrollment of minority groups in the colleges, or the establishment of courses of study relating to the cultures of minority groups.

As another example, you might find yourself involved in an argument over military action by our country in the defense of a small country in Asia which is being attacked by a neighboring country for the purpose of overthrowing its government and establishing a Communist government in its place which would be closely allied with the government of the invaders.

If you oppose our participation in that conflict, you might do so because you favor the Communist cause and would like to have the invading country succeed, or you might *oppose* our action there because you are of draft age and don't want to be drafted for military duty. However, these are not very admirable reasons, and you should try to think of one that would be more acceptable.

Another possibility is that you feel we should not sacrifice our lives and resources to defend a little country which is half a world away. This is a more respectable reason than the other two, but it is still not in keeping with the idealism of the American people. A better reason would be to maintain that our action there is illegal or immoral, and this should be the basis for your argument. This will give a moral tone to your comments and make them much more appealing to your listeners. You should stress such a reason from the start, because otherwise people will ascribe one of the less honorable motives to your argument.

In building up a reputation for reasonableness, it is not always necessary to have solutions for the problems at issue. It may be sufficient merely to show a sympathetic recognition of them. This principle was illustrated in one of the early *Amos and Andy* radio programs, in which Andy was giving a political speech. When he got to the subject of taxes he said, "Now about taxes. You take the taxes of the last 200 years, and you take the taxes of today, and there you has got 'em."

The same technique was used several years ago by a president of the United States in the course of his travel by train from Pueblo, Colorado westward into Utah. During a short stop in Grand Junction, Colorado, he came out on the back platform of the train to speak to the crowd waiting to see him. He mentioned traveling along the Arkansas and Gunnison Rivers that day and added, "I can see that what you people of Colorado need is water."

That was *all* he said. He didn't promise to get them more water, nor propose any method by which it could be obtained. In fact, there was nothing to propose, because the people of Colorado had already taken action to get as much water from these two rivers as it was then practical to obtain, but his comment drew a thundering applause from the crowd.

This is a technique which is especially effective

for a politician to use. If you are running for office, you should avail yourself of every opportunity to tell the unemployed that society should provide work for all who want it, to assert to groups of the retired that it is a shame that their life savings should be dissipated by the high property taxes they have to pay, and to express regret that the men you meet with Ph.D. degrees are not given work which is in keeping with their abilities. It is not necessary that you have plans for rectifying these inequities, or even that you should be running for an office that would have jurisdiction for solving these problems. To get the wholehearted support of the groups involved, it is enough that you should show that you are concerned!

2
Cutting Your Opponent Down to Size

Having established yourself as a person of sweet reasonableness, you should take advantage of every opportunity to diminish the credibility of your opponent. One of the most effective ways of doing this, as we have already pointed out, is to portray your opponent as a person of great argumentative skill who persuades people with eloquence rather than with sound arguments. This can be done, for example, by accusing an opponent of waiting until other people have expressed themselves on a subject before giving an opinion on it, either in order to get into a good argument by advocating the opposite point of view, or in order to "jump on the bandwagon" by adopting what appears to be the prevailing opinion about it. Such skill for arguing effectively on either side of any question, if it can be established, will impose a doubt upon your opponent's sincerity and reasonableness of his argument.

Such doubts can be raised, also, by describing

your opponent's arguments as the work of a skilled manipulator of facts. It is not enough that you should merely praise your opponent for speaking and argumentative skill, as Lincoln and Mark Antony did, but there should be a definite inference that the truth has been distorted. This inference, however, should not rest on a point-by-point refuation of your opponent's statements, because such detailed disputations regarding the facts often only lead to a mass of claims and counter-claims which leave the spectators uncertain as to what the truth is. It is better to attack your opponent's credibility by light-hearted, witty generalities.

For example, let us assume that you have just read the memoirs of a former officeholder in the United States government relating to his participation in the political events of his era, and that you disagree with his interpretation of those events. Instead of attempting a point-by-point refutation of his thesis, you may merely cast doubt on the accuracy of his account by saying, "With Mr._____, the manipulation of the facts of history has become a matter of art for art's sake. It radiates the professional talent of a skilled writer of fiction, and it does not always distort the truth. One cannot help admiring his originality and writing skill."

Again, you might say, "With him, it is not so much a matter of what actually happened, as what he believes he can persuade people to *believe* happened, and he was ever a man of sanguine faith."

A similar technique can be used to discredit an opponent by ascribing success in persuasiveness to political power or political skill rather than to sound ideas. For example, you may disagree with an action taken by a legislative committee in the state legislature. You can make that action seem the result of sinister machinations by a self-seeking political clique by saying, "We weren't quite a match for Senator _____'s bag of parliamentary tricks or for the pressure and funds which the _____ lobby was able to muster against us, this time."

Another effective way to discredit your opponent is to portray him as a person or member of a group that is lacking in goodness or in respectability. This lowers his standing in the estimation of your listeners, and causes them to give less credence to his arguments. Moreover, it is important to downgrade your opponent even if there is no one else listening, because this serves to put your opponent on the defensive and to weaken his self-confidence, making him less forceful in his arguments.

This is especially effective in arguments between husband and wife. In the course of the argument, bring to mind all of the culpable acts or omissions that may be charged, until your adversary feels completely inadequate. You may not get an admission of error, but this tactic should at least serve to change the subject, hopefully to one in which you are more sure of your ground!

Often you can attack your opponent's argument

as being reprehensible and disreputable, so as to turn it into a personal attack. For example, if he complains that the news media have not reported events fairly and objectively, accuse him of trying to *intimidate* the media and of denying them freedom of speech and of the press: If he asserts, as President Truman once foolishly did, that the Marine Corps has been asking for and getting more than its fair share of the defense budget, denounce him for having besmirched the fair name of the Marine Corps. If he says that your opposition to our nation's war policies gives aid and comfort to the enemy and impedes our efforts to get a negotiated peace, accuse him of striking below the belt in accusing you of being a traitor.

If you cannot find some obvious basis for discrediting your opponent on personal grounds, you may be able to accomplish this by attacking his family or his social background. For example, suppose a wife is trying to persuade her husband to lend some money to her brother, but he expresses doubt that he will ever get the money back. At this point she can say to him, "Oh, I suppose your family are all honest, upright people!" Then she should proceed to bring up every one of his "no-account" relatives, and point out how much beneath her he is in social status, and remind him how much she lowered herself to marry him. By the time she is through, he won't dare to mention her brother's poor credit rating again.

There are instances in which even your opponent's place of origin can serve to discredit him. Many years ago, before this country gave the Philippine Islands their independence, I heard a young Hawaiian give a speech in which he described how happy the Hawaiian people were to be a part of the United States, and suggested that the people of the Philippine Islands might be better off to request statehood in the United States rather than independence. A young Philippino in the audience obtained permission to speak a few words in rebuttal, and his most devastating argument was that the Hawaiian Islands were sinking into the sea and didn't matter anyway!

A similar means of discrediting an opponent was used by Senator John J. Ingalls of Kansas. When he was attacked on the floor of the Senate by Senator Eli Saulsburg of Delaware, Senator Ingalls disposed of the whole matter by saying, "I thank the gentleman from that great state, which has three counties at low tide and two counties at high tide, for his advice."

Another way of discrediting your opponent is to associate him with a group which is lacking in respectability. For instance, the only information I ever received as a boy regarding Democrats, Methodists, Adventists and Catholics, was that the Democrats were the type of people who wiped their noses on their sleeves; that the Methodists were a bunch of loud, hallelujah-shouting riff-raff, and that the Adventists and Catholics were just queer. So imbued had I become with these notions that I was surprised and puzzled when one of my Sunday-school teachers, a Presbyterian, told us that there was very little

difference between the Methodists and the Presbyterians in their beliefs. My puzzlement was further
increased by my mother's protestations that this was
not so, and that the Presbyterians were good,
respectable people, while the Methodists were rowdy
no-accounts. It was only after I left home and had had
personal contact with people of these maligned
groups that I learned what they really believed or
stood for.

In fact, almost any idea group with which you
might be in disagreement can be discredited by being
characterized by an undesirable stereotype, depending, of course, upon the prevailing viewpoint of
your audience. For example, the young, ultra-liberal
activists can usually be downgraded as "hippies,"
particularly if a large number of them affect long hair
and sloppy dress. On the other hand, those who
support the status quo against the clamoring of the
young activists can be dismissed as members of the
establishment. The ideas of these two groups can be
similarly disparaged as either the "crazy ideas of
youth," or the "old-fogy ideas of a worn-out generation."

If you are unable to downgrade the personality or
group of your opponent, you may achieve the same
result by disparaging the person or group being
promoted. It is often possible to dispose of an
argument on the basis of the personalities involved
without obtaining all of the facts about it. For
instance, we may have an incident in which a hippie-

type suspect is shot and killed by a law-enforcement officer while trying to escape arrest as a narcotics user and peddler. Government officials are investigating to determine whether the shooting was justified, and, in the meantime, you and many others have taken sides to debate the issue. If you take the side of the officer involved, you may justify his act on the basis of the disreputable character of the victim with some such argument as this: "Why all the sympathy for a dope pusher who was shot escaping arrest? A bank robber would not cause anyone a second glance and the item would be buried on page 2 for one day. This man was a much worse threat to society. It's because of the "bleeding hearts" in our midst that our valiant lawmen are hampered by overlenient laws and courts. Why don't they bleed a little for the thousands of youngsters condemned to a living death because of the vicious, greedy individuals like _____ who make millions on human agony?"

On the other hand, if you are arguing on the side of the victim, you may dispose of the question by referring to the law enforcement officers in the stereotyped role of cruel, sadistic bullies by saying: "By using storm trooper tactics, a group of fourteen peace officers were able to get one unarmed man by shooting him in the back. Well, peace officers, you have killed another hippie, another long-haired freak that was disturbing your society. You should be proud of yourselves, peace officers. You have some-thing to tell your grandchildren. You're big men now."

The same type of personal disparagement can be used to discredit an officeholder or a candidate for political office whom your opponent is advocating. If you cannot find anything in the officeholder's or candidate's political beliefs or policies to criticize him for, you may be able to undermine him by derogatory comments about his personality or character. Try to picture him as disagreeable, uncouth, or unmannered, which is much more effective than portraying him as merely immoral. Suggest that he and his wife are having domestic difficulties. Recount his displays of temper. If he is from the South or Midwest, allude to his crude western accent and his country manners, and if he is not a graduate of Harvard, Princeton, or Yale, refer to his lack of culture. A statement similar to the following could serve this purpose: "Mr. _____'s boorishness, selfrighteousness, poor diction, and irritating manners are well known, and are an important factor in his unpopularity with the voters. Can you imagine inviting him to dinner and having him sit at your table, smiling benignly, saying 'Mah friends,' and scratching himself?"

In like manner, you can often weaken your opponent's argument by attacking the reliability or the worth of a person he has quoted as an authority. For example, I once heard a debate in which one of the participants quoted a statement by a Mr. W_____ B_____, whom he identified as an economist. His opponent was able to destroy the effectiveness of this quotation by pointing out that Mr. W_____ B_____ was a socialist.

Another effective way of undermining your opponent's argument is to explain his ideas as growing out of his background or interests. For example, if he argues for social legislation benefitting the working people, point out that as the son of a workman, he would naturally favor this legislation. If, on the other hand, he argues against such legislation, point out that not having experienced economic want, he does not understand the problems of the working people. If he clamors for stricter laws to regulate or prohibit gambling, pornography or prostitution, or the use of alcohol or marijuana, ascribe this to his strict religious upbringing. If he opposes busing of school children to achieve racial balance in the schools, accuse him of being prejudiced against blacks. If he is an intellectual but favors socialism, speculate about why an intellectual would take this position, since he should expect to do better under capitalism where his superior ability would be recognized; but then happily remember that intellectuals like to play important roles in social movements, and that advocating socialism provides an outlet for this urge.

A similar effect may be achieved by ascribing opposing opinions or actions to a lack of experience or training in the area in question. For example, if you disagree with certain military policies of our government, you may explain them in terms of inadequate backgrounds on the part of the cabinet officers responsible for them. This idea could be expressed as follows:

"Consider the case of the Secretary of Defense, Mr. L_____. As an able politician and administrator, he became the architect of the policy of scaling down this country's role in the war, and he has reinforced that policy by a scaled down military budget that has tended to preclude any other alternatives. But Mr. L_____ is a politician pure, and he has never done anything else. He based his scheme for scaling down our military actions on the *political* needs of the country and has left the strategic matters to the armed services. Far from getting the kind of strategic advice he needed for carrying on the war, he gathered about him a group of politically minded incompetents under Assistant Secretary _____ who understood the military aspects of the war no better than he did.

"Then there is our revered Secretary of State, Mr. R_____. He took office with little knowledge of foreign affairs, and he has not done the homework required to give him a grasp of detailed problems. Rather, he has tended to delegate to subordinates, and particularly to Under Secretary _____, who was inclined to follow the president's lead in looking to military solutions for international problems. Consequently, when the crisis came, the State Department had no major course of diplomatic action to propose."

Sometimes, when we are unable to invalidate an opponent's ideas by ascribing them to the influence of his background or experience, we can accomplish the same result by ascribing them to the influence of a third person. This is particularly true where the person in question is recognized as having good judgment generally, but has an idea which might be shown to have originated with someone else. You may disagree with the foreign policies of the President of the United States, while nevertheless recognizing that he has generally been considered to be effective in domestic affairs. Under these circumstances, you can make your own arguments seem more credible if you frankly acknowledge his success in domestic affairs, where his background and experience have served him in good stead, but attack his foreign policies as being the outworn, irrelevant ideas of his secretary of state. This idea could be expressed by saying:

"The president's competence was not altogether limited to domestic affairs. When he applied his own intelligence and experience, he was equally good in foreign affairs. But for the most part, his concept of foreign affairs reflected those of the State Department, which saw Communism as an all-embracing world conspiracy whose subtle manipulations could be seen in all world disorders. Accepting this premise, the president was led to require American intervention whenever there was insurrection anywhere in the world."

Another person's argument can similarly be discredited by finding some ulterior motive for what he is advocating. If he proposes a relaxation of the laws relating to marijuana, liquor, prostitution, or pornography, you might insinuate that he has taken this stand because he wishes greater freedom for *his personal enjoyment* of these vices. If he favors an antlerless-deer hunt or an extension of the deer-hunting season, suggest that he is placing his desire to hunt ahead of protecting wild game from extinction. If he opposes prayer in public schools, interpret his stand as evidence that he is against God and religion. If he opposes rezoning of a section of the city which would permit the location of new business there, assume that he is just trying to keep out competition; but, if he favors rezoning, assume that he has an interest in a business to be established there or has land to sell in the area to be rezoned. If he takes a stand as an office holder or a candidate for office which is popular with the public but which you oppose accuse him of "playing politics" or of taking this stand just for votes.

This same questioning of motives can be applied to a whole group of protagonists, or even to a whole nation. For example, if you oppose military actions in which our country is engaged, you may ascribe that action to our desire for war profits, or for jobs in war industries, or to the imperialistic ambitions of the leaders of this country to keep industrially undeveloped countries under our economic control.

This same situation can apply to the question of the fluoridation of drinking water. If you should take the negative side of this question, you might be concerned with the scarcity of information on its harmful effects while there is widespread approval of it among members of the medical profession. This would seem to disprove your position on this question, unless you could show that there was some ulterior motive behind the medical profession's almost complete endorsement. Fortunately there is evidence of such a motive in the fact that manufacturing processes, such as the production of aluminum, produce large quantities of fluorides as a byproduct which normally goes to waste, but which can be used for the fluoridation of water. You should stress this point to suggest that there is a sinister conspiracy between industry and the medical profession to promote fluoridation of water for profit. Then you can quote the few chemists, doctors, and dentists who oppose fluoridation to prove that it is really harmful.

This technique of belittling your opponent, his argument, or his cause can be more effective if mixed with humor. You can use some humorous name for what he is advocating, as was done a few years ago when the Wagner-Murray-Dingle Bill in Congress, which proposed a wide-scale expansion of the Social Security program, was referred to by its opponents as the "Dingle-Dangle Bill." Another method is to present an idea with a clever allegory. That is, you can illustrate men's tendency to accept an infringement on their liberties, describing how a frog will jump out of a kettle of boiling water unharmed, but will stay in a kettle of cold water that is being heated until he is finally scalded to death. Similarly, you can illustrate the fact that recipients of welfare programs may well end up by paying for their benefits themselves, by telling about the snake that was so long and so twisted about in the corn field that, when he encountered his tail, he began to eat it with relish, thinking it was the tail of some other snake.

Sometimes a clever story can be used to hold up a social or economic class to bantering ridicule. One of the most effective of these stories was one which was popularized by some of the militant farm organizations in the early decades of this century in connection with their political attacks on the banks and big money interests. According to this story, a farmer was to meet a banker he had not met before who was know to have a glass eye so perfectly made that few people could tell which eye was which. When he did correctly identify the glass eye after the visit, his friend asked him how he could tell, and he said, "Well, as I was talking to the banker, I noticed that in one eye there was a glint of human kindness, and I knew that must be the glass eye!"

Another story which has become popular in recent years pokes gentle fun at the great horde of tax collectors—federal, state, and local—which afflict the common man. In this story, a professional strong man performing at a carnival customarily concluded his act by crushing a firm, ripe apple in his hand and then offering a $100 prize to anyone who could get even one more drop of juice out of it. On one occasion, a skinny little man accepted the challenge and lo and behold, there came not one drop, but a stream of juice from the dried up pulp of the apple. In astonishment, the carnival strong man cried, "My, you're strong. Are you a professional strong man?"

"Oh, no," the little man replied. "I'm with the Internal Revenue Service."

Sometimes it is possible to discredit an opponent or his argument by a clever comment or cutting repartee during the course of a debate. A famous example of this occurred in a debate in 1860 between Bishop Wilberforce and T.H. Huxley on the theory of evolution, when Bishop Wilberforce turned to Huxley and asked, "Is it through your grandfather or grandmother that you claim your descent from a monkey?"

Another example is found in the story of how a preacher finally squelched a persistent layman in a public argument they had about Jonah. The layman had referred to Jonah's being swallowed by a whale, while the preacher had insisted that the animal involved was not a whale, but a big fish. Finally the preacher said, "Well, I'll tell you what I'll do. When I get to Heaven, I'll ask Jonah."

"Well, but what if Jonah didn't go to heaven?"

the layman asked.

"In that case," retorted the preacher, "you can ask him."

An example of clever repartee as a means of discomfiting an opponent is attributed to John Wilkes, and relates to his early years as a member of the British House of Commons. His brash promotion of new ideas brought on the enmity of the older members of Parliament, and one of them made an angry forecast that he would come to an untimely end, either on the gallows or as the victim of some horrible disease.

"Sir," Wilkes is reported to have replied, "that will depend on whether I embrace your principles or your mistress!"

These are only a few examples of ways in which you can belittle your opponent or his cause. Years of practice, together with the careful study of jokes from books and newspapers, should enable you, in time, to come up with techniques of your own for showing your opponent in an unfavorable light and lowering him in the estimation of other people. When you have become expert in this field, you will be well on the way to becoming an accomplished debater.

3
The Force of Authority

Having considered the role of personalities in arguments, it is appropriate that we now give some attention to the rules of logic; for, although it is true that people form their opinions for personal reasons, they require that arguments at least follow the form of logical reasoning.

There are two main types of logic: inductive, which moves from specific examples to reach general conclusions, and deductive, which applies general principles to reach conclusions relating to specific situations. It is the latter type which we shall consider now.

Deductive logic can be thought of as authoritative logic, since it is based on commonly accepted premises or the pronouncements of recognized authority. The successful use of deductive logic requires that you be on the alert to find and recognize some outside authority for whatever point of view you are presenting. For example, if you are asked by a group of teenagers why premarital sex is wrong, you need not try to satisfy them with rational reasons, which in this age of practical prophylactics and the pill would be difficult to do anyway, but you can simply dispose of the question by saying, "It's a sin." Usually, in the face of such an authoritative pronouncement, no rational explanation is needed or pertinent.

The authority on which deductive logic rests is of five types. First, there are premises which are regarded as obviously true, such as the propositions that there is a supreme being, that we have been put on earth for a purpose, that unselfishness is a virtue, and that men are born with natural rights.

If anyone has the audacity to question any of these premises, you can reinforce them by pointing out that men have always accepted them. You can mention, for example, that every society has believed in the existence of a supreme being, and that such a belief must thus be instinctive, planted in our consciousness by God himself. (While this statement regarding the universality of the belief in God is *not entirely true*, you may still state it as a generalization without being challenged.

The second type is the authority of writings which are accepted as being of "divine origin" and thus unquestionably true. In Christian societies such as ours, the Bible is generally so regarded, and you should thus be ready to quote the Bible as an authority whenever you can find a statement in it which supports your argument. There are some arguments to support the idea of the infallibility of the Bible, as I will show later, but they are usually unnecessary, or are needed only to reinforce your listener's wavering faith in it. If your opponent challenges your quotation, it will most likely be in regard to what the Bible says or means, and not whether it is true. You should maintain a sufficient familiarity with this book to guard against your opponent's finding a quotation in it which will contradict or nullify the quotation which you have to offer.

The third type of authority is the testimony of experts on the subject. Actually, a quotation from almost anyone can serve, since your opponent and other listeners will always be more impressed by a statement from a third person than from you, no matter how eloquent and expressive your own statement might be. So effective is such expert testimony, in fact, that people will often defer their own sense of taste to it, as was illustrated by the effectiveness of cigarette advertising a few years ago, which asserted that "Among tobacco experts, among men who know tobaccos best," a particular brand of cigarettes was preferred, two to one.

It is preferable, of course, to present a quotation from a person who is trained or experienced, but you need not be concerned, for example, if you are arguing on some economic question and the only quotation you can offer to support your position is one by a famous movie actor. People are impressed by the views of any prominent person, the more prominent the better, and will certainly be persuaded by what a movie actor has to say. Only hope, in that case, that your opponent does not know *another* movie actor with an opposing viewpoint!

This reference to expert opinion is particularly effective when the person whose opinion you cite is a person of authority over you and your opponent. If you are arguing with a fellow worker about the most effective way of carrying out a work operation, you can often dispose of his assertions by saying, "Well, Mr. ___ (the section supervisor) doesn't think so. And Mr. ___ (the division manager) doesn't think so." It is immaterial that the section supervisor and the division manager might not have made a final decision on the question, or that they might even be looking to you and your opponent for suggestions about it. The fact that they had once expressed themselves in favor of your viewpoint will usually be sufficient to discourage your opponent from pursuing the matter further.

Next is the type of authority referred to as the general consensus, the force of family or social tradition. It expresses itself most commonly in such statements as, "This is contrary to the American way of life;" or, "We don't believe that;" or "We Hunsingers have been Republicans for five generations." It is perhaps the most important authority of all in relation to human conduct, and it manifests itself in the compunctions which prevent us from speaking lightly of motherhood, our country, or the U.S. Marines. It is also the kind of authority which proclaims that no man who is a real man and a gentleman will ever turn down a challenge to a fight, or refuse a proffered alcoholic drink, or fail to tip a waitress, bellhop, barber, or taxi driver who has served him.

The fifth type of authority is similar to the fourth, in that it represents the general consensus, but it expresses itself in common sayings or adages. Like quotations from the Bible or other religious writings, however, there are examples which can be called upon to substantiate almost any point of view, as is illustrated by the following pairs of adages:

A rolling stone gathers no moss.
The rambling bee gathers the honey.

You can't teach an old dog new tricks.
A man is never too old to learn.

He who hesitates is lost.
Look before you leap.

Don't put all your eggs in one basket.
Jack of all trades, master of none.

The feathers make the bird.
Beauty is only skin deep.

Birds of a feather flock together.
Opposites attract.

Two heads are better than one.
Too many cooks spoil the broth.

Nothing ventured, nothing gained.
A bird in the hand is worth two in the bush.

Haste makes waste.
Procrastination is the thief of time.

Absence makes the heart grow fonder.
Out of sight, out of mind.

It is important, if you expect to be an effective debater, to keep a good fund of these adages in mind to recall whenever one can be quoted to support your point of view. Take a chance that your opponent will not be able to recall a conflicting one.

The force of deductive premises rests on the fact that they not only carry the conviction of ultimate truth but also bear the power of moral sanction. This is illustrated by the popular story of a man who was being out-argued in a religious discussion by two smart-aleck young men, and who finally said, "Well, boys, you might out-argue me, but you can't out-believe me."

The import of this story is that the older man's unquestioning loyalty to the religious beliefs he had been taught was a virtue, and that the brash rationalization of the young men was a great wickedness. Indeed, this idea has ever been the great sustaining force of all religions. The Old Testament kings who "did evil in the sight of the Lord" displayed their wickedness, in most cases, only in their rejection of the religious teachings and advice of the prophets, and the present-day religious leaders similarly pronounce a lack of faith to be the greatest evil as well as a cause for the loss of salvation.

Similar moral judgments serve to enforce other authoritative concepts. For example, the philosophies of the bully and the bigot have found support in popular concepts which brand a man as a renegade, a coward, a skinflint, or a goody-goody, if he fails to live up to them. So strong is the acceptance of these moral judgments that few have the courage to defy them. Many a man has faced certain death at the hands of a professional gunman rather than face the possibility of being adjudged a coward by his friends, who, he knew, would make such a judgment, even though they were sympathetic toward him and appreciative of his dilemma.

It is this particular force of deductive logic which you must keep in mind if you are to become really expert in the art of argument. You should never weaken a deductive argument by trying to explain it on a rational basis, because a *deductive premise does not rest on reason.* At all costs, you should never attempt to argue with a rationalist on his own terms. Instead, if you are relying on a deductive argument, invoke the authority on which it rests. Since you are arguing from a popularly accepted premise, you have the weight of evidence on your side, and your opponent, if he disagrees, must bear the burden of proof. You should see that he does so. If he argues that there is no Hell, ask him if he can be sure there is no such place. Since this is a question which cannot be positively proved one way or the other, he will have to admit that you could be right.

The best argument to use in support of a deductive premise is the one used by Lord Peter in Swift's *A Tale of a Tub*, in response to his brothers' expressions of doubt that the slices of bread he had served them were really slices of mutton. "Look ye, Gentlemen," he said, "to convince you what a couple of blind, positive, ignorant, wilful puppies you are, I will use but this plain argument; By G___, it is true, good, natural Mutton as any in Leaden-Hall Market; and G___, confound you both eternally if you offer to believe otherwise." As Swift pointed out: "Such a thundering Proof as this left no farther Room for Objection."

In instances in which this threat of damnation would not apply or would be ineffective, you can still apply the moral sanctions of a deductive premise to win your argument. If your opponent expresses doubts about the Bible or the tenets of Christianity, tell him that this is the voice of the Devil speaking to him, and insinuate that his rejection results from his unwillingness to accept the moral teachings of the church or to subject himself to the will of God in the conduct of his life. Also, associate disbelief with immorality by pointing out how the young people are rejecting Christianity and are indulging in illicit sex and drugs and riotous living. If your opponent is from a wealthy and influential family but espouses the cause of the working people, denounce him as a traitor to his class. If he declines to settle a question under discussion by resorting to fisticuffs, insinuate that he is a coward. If he espouses the civil rights of blacks, call him a "nigger-lover." If he has conscientious scruples about participating in the pledge of allegiance to the flag because of its inclusion of the phrase, "under God," suggest that he is disloyal to his country and probably a Communist. If he declines a friendly drink, grill him for a half-hour to find out what crazy religion or social crusade he might be affiliated with that would make him so unsociable and goody-goody. If he argues against the practice of tipping as an inequitable or degrading custom, tell him about some people you know who are so stingy and gauche that they never leave a tip.

The use of deductive logic is well illustrated by the advice which an old experienced lawyer once gave to a young one. He said, "If the facts are against you, pound on the law; if the law is against you, pound on the facts; and if the facts and the law are both against you, pound on the table." So, in the general field of argument we may say, "If the force of authority is against you, argue in terms of the facts or of reason; if the facts or reason are against you, argue in terms of recognized authority; and if authority, the facts, and reason are all against you, just try to outshout your opponent."

4
Begging the Question

There is a special kind of deductive logic known as "begging the question." It differs from ordinary deductive logic in that, instead of a direct statement that an idea is unquestionably true, there is merely an assumption that it is true or an assertion of its truth by an indirect statement. It derives its name from the fact that it assumes as true the very idea which is at issue. For example, you may be having an argument about the proper way for a man to comb or part his hair. When your opponent presses you for the reason for your preference, you can simply say, "I want my hair combed right."

A classic example of begging the question is found in the familiar story of an evangelist's retort to one of his hecklers during a sermon. In this sermon, the evangelist became inpassioned in his lurid description of the terrors of Hell, when one man in the audience said, "Oh, I don't believe there is any Hell."

"Well," said the preacher, "you will *when you get*

there!"

Another example can be found in the current controversy over court procedures in criminal cases. In a cerain case, pertinent evidence against the accused may be ruled by the court to be inadmissible because of the probability that it would unduly prejudice the jury and produce an erroneous verdict, and the case is subsequently dismissed for want of sufficient evidence. Upon the dismissal of the case, the defendant is freed of the charges and is presumed to be innocent.

However, if you are opposed to the rules of evidence which were applied in this case and feel that the criminals are being coddled by the courts, you might assume that this defendant was really guilty and argue that, "criminals such as he should not be allowed to escape just punishment because of a technicality of the law." Other familiar examples of begging the question are:

"A man who would *commit such a vicious crime* as that doesn't deserve a trial."

"Yes, I think he is entitled to a fair trial, even if he is a *murderer*."

"I say let's hang him now without a trial, and put a stop to this type of *organized crime*. We should let the *rustlers* know we won't put up with their activities any longer."

"I don't take the word of any *lying, thieving* Indian."

"I agree he has a right to his *cockeyed* opinion."

"We shouldn't be intolerant of him just because he happens to be a *dirty, worthless, no-account s.o.b.*"

"I don't believe we should support our government when it is *in the wrong.*"

"One man who is *more right* than his neighbors is a majority of one."

"We should put the government in the hands of the *more intelligent.*"

Begging the question is generally more effective than ordinary deductive logic because, by being stated indirectly, it does not invite a challenge as does a directly-stated proposition, and being presented with off-hand casualness, it bears an air of assurance which makes it seem unquestionably true. Thus, if a candidate for office should assert that there is waste or corruption in the present government or that undeserving people are receiving welfare, or that the rich are not paying a fair share of taxes, he would be expected to support them with evidence.

However, if he promises to *abolish* the wastes, or see that no one gets welfare payments that he is not entitled to, or will see that Gov. ___'s millionaire friends pay taxes like anyone else, the implied charges of corruption in the present government will be accepted without question. Similarly, if you say that women are poor drivers, you will probably get into an argument about it, particularly if there are women present; but if you say that a tree will stand and grow in one place for two hundred years, and then suddenly jump in front of a woman driver, the implied criticism will go unchallenged!

Other effective means of discrediting by indirect reference are the use of such statements as, "I believe our party can *call this country back* to the greatness that is in us," or "I want to *restore* our nation's prestige," or "I call upon the people to *return* to the old-fashioned virtues of hard work and integrity."

Such an indictment of present conditions or of persons presently in power can be especially effective if you can tie the indictment in with popular prejudices, such as the fear of the power of the Federal government.

For example, in a state in which the local school districts were extensively controlled by state laws and regulations, the state superintendant of schools successfully opposed the acceptance of increased federal aid to education in the state by proposing to give control of education *back to the people*. Similarly, a candidate for a federal office who proposed the abolition of certain direct social programs, such as low-cost housing, and the direct substitution of private initiative for those programs through the encouragement of tax incentives, was able to gain active support for his proposal by suggesting that we "restore the government to the people."

This technique of implying one fact by stating another can be particularly effective in the field of advertising. For example, the statement: "We sell for less," implies that although the price is less, the quality is just as good. Similarly, the statements, "What a whale of a difference a few cents make," "Accept no substitutes," and "Read what leading critics say," provide the implication that the products in question are *better* than rival products.

In similar fashion, you can often voice a serious doubt about a rival group or product by merely making a simple statement about your own. A statement, for instance, that your product "contains lanolin," or is "made from pure Pennsylvania crude oil" implies, without the need for explaining how or why, that these ingredients make the products *better*. People will assume that this is so, because otherwise you would not have mentioned these ingredients.

In the same way, if in a television advertisement a woman says, "I like ___ hospital insurance because it permits me to have the doctor of my choice," it gives a strong implication, not necessarily true, that other hospital insurance plans do not give patients that choice. Likewise, if a candidate for office makes a point of promising that, if elected, he "will look after the voter's interests," he can implant the idea, without any explanation or elaboration, that the incumbent has not been doing these things. An office-seeker whose opponent happens to be a school teacher can merely state that he is *not a teacher*, in order to establish the idea that being a teacher is somehow disqualifying. So, too, a political campaigner can inpugn the sincerity of the opposing party's candidate by declaring, "We need jobs, not rhetoric! Vote for ___."

Another effective way of begging the question is simply to ask a question about the point at issue. We are all familiar with the joke of asking a man if he still beats his wife; but the same effect can be achieved seriously by asking such a question as, "Are the ___s about to be separated?" or "Did ___ father an illegitimate child?" It is not necessary that these questions have any basis in fact. People will assume an affirmative answer from the mere fact of your having asked the questions.

Questions can be even more effective if we ask why something is so, instead of asking *whether* it is so. This implies that the facts have already been established. For instance: "Why do proponents of water fluoridation sidestep its cumulative hazards?" and, "Why are people with Ph.D.'s and masters degrees getting food stamps?"

A similar effect can be obtained by asking a question which by its very wording assumes its truth. The use of such a question was illustrated in a recent interview with a professed atheist by a newspaper reporter. The atheist, a woman, was telling about a dangerous airplane ride during which many of the passengers had prayed for a safe landing. She was asked, "With you on the plane, do you think the Lord would have answered anyone's prayers?" The woman had already said that she did not believe there was any God, but this question assumed that she did, and it was a question she could not answer directly without admitting that God existed.

Adlai Stevenson became the victim of such a question when he first ran for president, on the Democratic ticket, to follow the Democratic incumbent, Harry Truman. The Republicans claimed that Truman had made a mess of running the government, and Stevenson was asked during the campaign whether he thought he could clean up the mess in Washington.

This was a question which called for a simple yes or no answer, but either answer would be damaging to Mr. Stevenson's candidacy. If he answered "no," he would be admitting an inability to administer the government efficiently, but if he answered "yes," as he actually did, he would be admitting that the previous Democratic president *had* made a mess of running the government, and he would bear the onus of that judgment as the Democratic party's new candidate. On the other hand, if he had answered the question by saying that he did not necessarily agree that the government was in a mess, he would have put himself on the defensive, and would have left himself open to the charge that he couldn't even recognize inefficiency in government when he saw it.

Sometimes you can make a derogatory implication about a person or group by simply expressing doubt that something worse is true about them. This is illustrated by the joke about the man who told his friend about coming to the friend's defense against scurrilous comments by others. "They were saying," he said, "that you were not fit to associate with hogs, but I told them I thought you were." Another example is found in the testimony before a Congressional Committee in which a witness described a named group as Communists. When pressed as to whether a certain person in that group was a Communist, the witness said, "I do not know whether Mr. ___ was a *card-carrying Communist* or not." Here the emphasis on the "card-carrying" left a strong implication that the man in question was some kind of Communist, even though perhaps not a card carrying one.

Another form of begging the question can be found in the mere choice of the words we use to describe what we are talking about, as is illustrated by a schoolboy's distinctions between a war and a massacre, and between caution and cowardice. In the one case the boy is reported to have said, "If the white men kill the Indians, it's a war, but if the Indians kill the white men, it's a massacre." In the other case the boy said, "Caution is when you are afraid, and cowardice is when the other fellow is afraid."

In like manner, depending on one's position and point of view, distinctions can be made between *enthusiasm* and *fanaticism, bravery* and *foolhardiness, frank-*

ness and *tactlessness, helpfulness* and *officiousness, self-confidence* and *conceit, liberty* and *license, determination* and *stubbornness, sympathy* and *sentimentality, leniency* and *laxity, thrift* and *stinginess, planning* and *scheming, righteous wrath* and *hotheadedness,* and *loyalty* and *servility.*

Indeed, we can often indicate at the onset whether an idea or event is good or bad simply by the way we refer to it. Let us suppose an incident in which several Protestant ministers espoused the cause of Communism and you were called on to write a newspaper headline to cover it. If you believed in Communism yourself, you would probably write, "Protestant Ministers Embrace Communism," However, if you did not approve of Communism, you would possibly say, "Communists Infiltrate Ranks of Protestant Clergy," or, better yet, "Protestant Ministers Become Dupes of Communists."

Similarly, people who favor welfare legislation talk about the social security "program," while those who are opposed to it call it a social security "scheme." What one group calls a "soil bank," another calls a "subsidy." Those who approve of a provision of a tax law refer to it as a "tax benefit," while others call it a "tax loophole." People who oppose the construction of a new building for the Welfare Department may refer to it as a "handout heaven," or a "mini-palace," or a "mini Taj Mahal," or a "junior-grade Pentagon."

This use of words to give favorable or unfavorable connotations to ideas can apply to descriptive words or phrases, as well as to the choice of names. One newspaper reporter expressed his feelings about atheism by referring to a well-known atheist as a "self-confessed" atheist, and another expressed his judgment of a witness before the Unamerican Activities Committee by reporting that this person had "admitted" knowing all but one of the persons named on a list of subversives. In a third instance, in reporting an event in which a grown woman had struck her aged father in an argument, a reporter conveyed the idea of the enormity of her act by saying that the woman had struck her "own" father. In still another case, a debater was able to cast doubt upon the idea of Right-to-Work laws by referring to them as the "so-called Right-to-Work laws." On the other hand, the use of the term, "right-to-work," in connection with these laws was, itself, a happy choice of language, in that it suggested, to those who did not know better, that these laws would guarantee employment to all who desired it. In similar fashion the use of the term "free enterprise" for Capitalism is appealing because it suggests that people have more freedom under this system than under other economic systems; and the term "People's Republic" suggests that such a government is somehow more representative of the people than other republics.

Another effective way of begging the question is simply to place your opponent in the playing role of the type of person you represent him to be. In a sense, you are begging the question whenever you present a

Negro in a play or story as a shiftless, lazy person, or show a Jew as grasping, or describe a German as arrogant or stubborn, because such a presentation assumes that all representatives of such a group fall within a general stereotype.

However, you can make this role-playing technique even more effective if you can present a character in the role of your argumentative opponent, himself, and have *him* profess adherence to the unpopular ideas or attitudes which you insist that the opposing group holds. A good example of this is found in a recent proposal that homosexuals be barred from teaching positions. The proponents of this proposal argued that homosexual teachers would try to induct their pupils into their homosexual practices, but their opponents responded that there was no reason why homosexuals would be any more inclined to try to corrupt the morals of children than anyone else, and that, in fact, most of the known cases of child molestation or of contributing to the delinquency of minors involved adults who were *heterosexual*. However, the proponents of the ban seemed to turn the tide of public opinion in their favor when they discontinued their direct arguments on this point, and instead presented a series of spot announcements on the radio in which the speaker said: "I'm a homosexual teacher, and I'm proud of it. That doesn't mean that *all* of my pupils will become homosexuals. That's their choice to make."

One of the most effective ways of begging the

question is to associate what your opponent likes or advocates with something that is distasteful or undesirable, or to identify what you advocate with something recognized as desirable. Some good examples are:

Anyone who likes that would suck eggs.

If you favor clean air, clean water, and natural foods, you will like ___."

We have an obligation to preserve the American way of life.

I propose to go on in faith and loyalty to the traditions of our race.

Four score and seven years ago, our fathers brought forth on this continent a new nation....

Who is here so rude that would not be a Roman? If any, speak, for him have I offended.

This association of an idea with what is recognized as good or bad can often be brought about by pointing out who is in favor of it and who is opposed to it. Thus, you can bring disfavor upon a new plan for public welfare by pointing out that the Soviet Union has such a plan in operation, or you might aid the promotion of the Equal Rights Amendment to the

Constitution, as members of the women's liberation movement recently did, by mentioning that the Ku Klux Klan opposed it. If you are talking to a group of working people about some proposed labor legislation, you can greatly enhance your cause by pointing out that the labor unions favor it and that the big-business organizations oppose it. Likewise, if you are discussing a proposed anti-obscenity law with a church group, you can say that a well-known "flesh" magazine contributed thousands of dollars to a campaign fund to defeat it.

Similarly, we can enhance the effectiveness of an idea by the way we categorize it in terms of general political or economic theory. The label "liberal," for instance, is quite popular today, particularly among the younger generation, and it is desirable to classify your ideas as liberal if this can be done. This does not require a great deal of logic or consistency, as these labels tend to change in the course of time. For example, after World War I, the idea of our membership in the League of Nations and our participation in world affairs to maintain world order and prevent aggression between nations was considered "liberal" philosophy, while the spirit of isolation which opposed it was regarded as "conservative." However, today, the people who favored our involvement in Viet Nam to act under an international treaty to protect South Viet Nam from outside aggression have been referred to as "conservatives"; while the people who oppose such involvement, and who generally advocate a lesser role for this country in international affairs, are spoken of as "liberals." The secret is to beat your opposition to the label you prefer for your idea, and, once you have established it, they must accept the opposite designation.

A similar technique is to place the idea or practice you oppose in a class with other ideas or practices which are recognized as being undesirable. You can argue against abortion or other means of birth control, or against capital punishment or war by simply saying that "these acts constitute murder, and everyone knows that murder is wrong!"

Another such possibility is to label an organization which you oppose as a Communist organization. Then you can point out that Communist organizations advocate the overthrow of non-Communist governments by force, and sanction other acts of terrorism and violence to carry out their ends. This will establish the organization in question as one which advocates terrorist methods of operation without the need of specific evidence that it does so in fact.

Similar results can be obtained by categorizing an organization or a proposal as Fascist or Socialist. Let us suppose that someone has proposed a plan for government-administered health insurance, which you oppose. You can discredit the plan by calling it socialized medicine, a term generally associated with Great Britain, and point out how the British health services have suffered from their lack of modern hospital facilities, a lack of trained doctors, and the lack of doctor incentives under the British plan of assigning patients to doctors. It is not necessary to indicate how the plan proposed for this country would involve these same difficulties.

Another possibility relates to the legalization of marijuana. You can oppose such legislation effectively by discussing marijuana in association with other drugs and then describing the dangers of drug use generally and the harrowing details of people jumping to their deaths from high windows under the delusions experienced in LSD trips, or turning to a life of crime and degradation to gratify their addiction to heroin, being careful not to be too specific about what drug was involved. Having placed marijuana in the same class with these other drugs, you can seem to impute the dangers of these other drugs to it.

One effective way of identifying your point of view with popular ideas is to assume that people generally agree with you about it. This can often be done by prefacing your remarks with a statement such as, "As you know," or "You will certainly agree that___," or "As a government employee, you are aware that___." Having been taken into your confidence in this way, others will be reluctant to disagree with you for fear that they will offend you or that you will think them stupid.

Another way is to ignore the basic question and simply confine your comments to the question of how the adoption of the policy can be prevented, or how its consequences can be minimized, or how the authorities can be persuaded to modify or rescind it, or how we may avoid such mistakes in the future. Some good examples are:

> These developments overseas have afforded the vice-president an excellent opportunity to break with the administration's war policies in his bid for the presidency.
>
> Fortunately, there are available legislative means for heading off such a disaster. The Senate need only add on an amendment that the legislation go into effect only insofar as it does not conflict with the Constitution.
>
> Local demonstrations are being initiated throughout the country in the hopes of conveying to elected officials the communities' feelings about the war.
>
> If we are to avoid similar ill-fated involvements in the future, there must be a more realistic understanding of our international rights, responsibilities, and powers.

Sometimes an impression of great popularity of your viewpoint can be given by implying that there has been a shift in sentiment toward it, even though many people honestly thought otherwise before. This can be expressed by such sentences as, "We believe the president will respond to the growing sense of frustration with the course of these negotiations," or

"History will record that we were right," or "Even those who still believe we were morally right in intervening in that conflict, now agree that we paid too high a price," or "Even long-time liberals are beginning to have doubts about the effectiveness of much of the new social legislation."

This technique is especially effective because it permits the other person to agree with you without losing face for having previously expressed an opposing idea.

This impression of general popularity can also be produced by an implication of popular demand. This can be expressed in such statements as:

Since only a limited number will be admitted, you are urged to make your reservations early.

The thing people like about ___ is ___.

The leadership of ___ was achieved through ___.

To meet the constantly growing demand for ___,

If your druggist is sold out, write to ___.

Doesn't the opinion of hundreds of women count for anything?

Every article merits the confidence of you who, year after year, rely on the ___ label.

The same effect can be obtained by referring to the idea argued against as the opposite of something universally approved. For example, you can argue effectively against Communism by treating it in terms of Communism versus Democracy, or Communism versus Christianity, instead of Communism versus Capitalism, which presents the true opposites. Likewise, you can present the theory of evolution in an unfavorable light by describing it as "man's story of creation," or "the Devil's story of creation," in contrast with "God's story of creation" as presented in the Book of Genesis.

Indeed, almost any point of view can be identified with some favorable concept, and in many cases both sides of a controversy can identify with the same beneficial objective. Thus, racial segregationalists and anti-segregationalists both justify their stands on the basis of the right of association; the proponents and opponents of our military action in Viet Nam have both stated their arguments in terms of the right of self-determination for the Vietnamese; and the proponents and opponents of prayers in public schools have both argued in terms of religious liberty, with the proponents claiming the right to a *voluntary* exercise of their religious beliefs in public, and the opponents claiming a right not to have religious beliefs and practices *imposed* on them by the government.

Similarly, it is often possible for both sides of an

argument to ascribe the same faults and weaknesses to each other, as when the advocates of Socialism and Capitalism both denounce the opposing doctrine as "materialistic," and when an ultra-rightist, preaching the doctrine of Americanism and stirring up ill feeling among and toward "foreign" groups, pleads for the elimination of hate and dissension between his political group and other "American" groups.

Another effective means of begging the question is simply to refuse to take your opponent seriously. Become indignant at his statements, as if his ideas were preposterous, or respond to them with surprise and disbelief. A statement such as, "Is that so?" or, "I didn't know that to be the case," or "I've never heard it put that way before," or "You're the first person I've known to put it so strongly," or "That's news to me," will often give your opponent pause and cause him to reconsider his position. The same effect can be obtained by expressing doubt or amazement about the policies of someone else your opponent is defending, with a statement such as, "The administration's foreign policy defies understanding."

Another similar technique is to assume that your opponent doesn't really mean what he says. To do this, you can respond to his argument with, "You're kidding," or "Don't be silly," or "All joking aside," or "Now let me tell one," or "Surely you don't mean that," or "That statement is not worthy of you," or "You're too fine a person to really believe that," or "If I didn't know you better, I'd believe you meant it!"

If you are in a public debate, you can show the ridiculousness of your opponent's argument by saying that you can never tell when he is joking, because when he acts as if he is telling a joke, he isn't funny, but when he seems to be serious, he often *is* funny. You can point out to the audience that there is a way that they can tell, because you have noticed that when your opponent intends to tell a joke, he has a habit of stepping forward and pausing slightly just before delivering the punch line, and that is a signal for them to laugh politely.

The ultimate effect of begging the question can be seen when a basic assumption can be made regarding a situation which can color its whole interpretation and make the facts seem different.

Let us assume from these facts a situation in which a group of men, all Negroes are inmates of a prison. While there, they are indicted for murder in connection with the killing of a prison guard. To complete the situation, before the men can be brought to trial for killing the guard, one of them is killed in a prison riot. On the face of it, this seems like a case in which a convicted criminal has been slain in an attempted prison break. However, if you take note of the fact that he was a Negro and a member of one of the Negro activist groups, and that this imprisonment was initially connected with the Negroes' struggles for civil rights, the situation becomes altogether different. The man then becomes a *political* prisoner instead of a *criminal*, and his imprisonment, indictment for murder, and

Carlos L. Hunsinger | 73
slaying become manifestations of the white man's oppression. In discussing this man's fate, you can refer to him as a martyr and a man of great compassion who understood the prejudices of people who had persecuted him and would be happy to know that his death had served the cause of black men's liberties.

As another example, let us assume that there is a small Asiatic country which was given its independence by a colonial power after World War II; that the treaty granting independence to the country divided it into two separate nations because Communist forces had already set up a government in the one part without elections, and the other part wanted to be free to establish a non-Communist government; that the former later attacked the latter to reunite the two nations under one Communist government; and that our country, at the request of the assailed nation and in accordance with previous treaty obligations, came to its defense.

At first glance, this seems to be a situation in which our country took military action to preserve world order and prevent international aggression. However, if you take note of the fact that the two countries initially involved in this conflict were originally one, and that the country under attack also contains a group of Communists, you can make an overall assumption that this is a civil war, which gives an entirely different appearance to the situation. The United States becomes the aggressor, interfering with the internal affairs of a small nation striving for unity and independence.

This assumption regarding our military role in this situation involves another: If newspaper, radio, and television accounts of this conflict uniformly describe the country with the Communist government as the aggressor, in contrast to information received from Communist sources, you can maintain your position that the United States is the aggressor if you assume that our prominent newspapers and radio and television networks are tools of U.S. "imperialism" and are not reporting the facts correctly.

These three special assumptions are effective because, although they are not necessarily representative of the general views of the situations involved, they do bear an air of plausibility. We do know that Negroes have often been subjected to oppressive and tyrannical treatment at the hands of law enforcement officials in this country, that industrial nations such as ours have at times interfered in the internal affairs of undeveloped nations to further their own economic or political aims, and that news media have sometimes slanted or distorted the news. Thus, any assumption based on a recognition of these social wrongs will find ready acceptance with many people.

Of course, you will have to ignore certain facts, such as that the Negro prisoner's *original* arrest and *conviction* were for a crime that had nothing to do with the civil rights movement, that the attacking force and the victims of the attack in Asia were in fact separated under the peace treaty which granted their independence into two different countries, divided by a well-defined demilitarized zone; and that it is inconceivable that all of the representatives of the news media, coming from every walk of life and every social and economic background, could be brought into a conspiracy to distort the truth.

However, most people will not think to bring up these facts. If they do, you can ignore them, but avail yourself of every opportunity to repeat your argument. Eventually, people will give up trying to point out the inconsistencies in your position, and many, influenced by the repetition of your assertions, will come to accept your point of view. It is not necessary, in this regard, that the basic assumption of your argument be logical. In fact, the more notorious, and the more unreasonable in its radicalism it is, the more publicity it will receive and the more public sympathy it is likely to gain.

Indeed, if such an assumption is stated positively enough and with enough assurance, it can overcome positive evidence to the contrary or even make contrary evidence serve as evidence of its own truth. This was illustrated in Senator Joseph McCarthy's investigation of Communism several years ago, in which he alleged that the Democratic administration then in office was "soft on communists," and that the government was infiltrated with communists. One of the departments of government which he investigated was the State Department, and a committee headed by Senator Millard Tydings of Maryland was appointed to investigate this charge. When this committee reported that it found no evidence of Communists in the State Department, the followers of Senator McCarthy, hotly proclaimed that this was more evidence that the administration and the party in power *were* soft on Communists. Senator McCarthy's branding of this report as a "whitewash" was largely responsible for Tydings's defeat when he sought re-election.

We find a similar illustration in the case of a small revolutionary political party which claimed to represent the people in the new, developing nation in which it was formed, but justified its activist practices on the ground that the party in power *controlled the elections* and would prevent a democratic expression of the people's will. Upon the decisive defeat of this revolutionary party in a later election, its followers were able to cite this fact as proof that the election had, in fact, been rigged.

In another instance, students of archeology found records of ancient stories of man's temptation and fall much older than the story of Adam and Eve, which tended to show that the Bible story was just a copy of an older folk legend and not divinely inspired. This failed to daunt the members of a certain fundamentalist religious group, which insisted that the Bible story was the word of God. Said one of its ministers, "See how the Devil works, planting a false story in men's minds to cause them to doubt the true, divine story."

In its final degree of effectiveness, a general assumption of this type can be used as the basis for asserting that the opposing viewpoint is founded on a false assumption, placing your opponents on the defensive. This is illustrated by the statement, "My opponent's argument seems to be based on the assumption that Satan is merely an allegorical figure, and not a real being," or by the commentary that "The administration's action is based on the outworn assumption that the attack was part of a world-wide Communist strategy to dominate the world, and that if we did not stop them, the other nations of Asia would fall like a row of dominoes." A similar pronouncement is implied in the comment of the Englishman after his return home from world travel, that "everywhere else in the world they drive on the wrong side of the road!"

Statements of the type which describe an opposing viewpoint as being based on a false assumption, if made with enough assurance, can often dispose of the whole question at issue, and make it unneccesary to go into the facts as to which assumption is really correct.

5
Arguing in a Circle

There is a third type of deductive logic known as "arguing in a circle." It is like ordinary deductive logic except that instead of having one major premise from which the conclusion of the argument will flow, it has two or more major premises which are not sufficient alone to support the conclusion, but which can support each other to do so.

A good example is that of the cowboy who refused to eat mutton because he said he didn't like it. When asked why he didn't like it, he said, "I don't know. I've just never eaten any." A humorous variation is about a man who disliked cabbage. He said, "I don't like cabbage, and I'm glad I don't, because if I did, I'd eat the darned stuff."

A similar example relates to a young man who dropped out of college to bum around the country in order to find himself. When he was asked why he couldn't find himself in college, he said, "Because college is not where it is happening. It's happening out there." Then when asked what was happening "out there," he said, "I don't know. That's what I have to find out."

The same type of reasoning was exhibited by a man who kept and fed a team of horses which were of no apparent use to him. When he was asked why he kept the horses, he said he needed them to cultivate and harvest the hay on a small plot of land he had; and when asked what he did with the hay, he said he needed it to feed his horses. It recalls the machinations of the dictator who initiated a program to increase the country's birth rate in order to acquire the manpower he needed for his military operations, which were designed, in turn, to gain living room for his country's large population.

In some cases, the two premises of an argument in a circle do not directly support each other, but mutually support a third premise upon which they both rest. This is illustrated by the argument of a young man in support of the efficacy of good luck charms. He was bragging about the lucky rabbit's foot he had when someone asked him, "Has it really brought you good luck?"

"Yes," he said, "Since I got it, I found a four-leaf clover."

There are many clever and effective arguments or reasons for doing things which do not exactly fit this pattern of being based on two or more mutually supporting premises, but which nevertheless have a backward twist to them which returns the conclusion to the starting point. One good example of this is of a man who believed that the fog horns were being used along the coast to keep the elephants from invading the land. When someone pointed out to him that there were no elephants in that area, he said, "Yes, the fog horns are effective, aren't they?"

Another such type of reasoning involved a man who was going to the bank to deposit a $100 cash bonus he had received and who agreed to deposit a similar $100 bonus for a friend. Later he reported to the friend that he had lost the friend's $100 bill on the way to the bank.

"How do you know it was my $100 you lost?" the friend asked.

"Because I still have mine," he replied.

This type of argument seems to be encountered most frequently in arguments between husbands and wives. In one case, a husband and wife were arguing about whether men or women were the more intelligent, and the husband was complaining that it was frustrating to try to argue with the wife because she didn't even understand what he was saying. She retorted, "That just goes to prove that women are more intelligent, because, if men were really intelligent, they'd know better than to try to argue with women."

In another case, a woman woke her husband to ask him if he was asleep yet. When he asked her why she had awakened him to ask him such a question, she said, "Because, if you weren't asleep, I wouldn't have had to wake you to ask you."

There is another variation of the technique of arguing in a circle which applies a different type of reasoning to the two sides of a question so as to get a favorable result for your point of view in either case. A Democratic candidate used an argument of this type in a recent election to challenge the findings of public opinion polls which were unfavorable to his party.

He said: "I don't believe the opinion polls that show that the Republicans are going to win by a landslide. For instance, these polls show the Democrats will lose California by over 1,000,000 votes, but an independent poll by the Democratic party showed that they would *win* in California by 3,000,000 votes. When two intelligent groups come up with that much difference, it is obvious that there is some irrational factor involved in conducting these polls. Therefore, I reject the polls favoring the Republicans."

By such a statement, this candidate seemed to be arguing successfully both ways in regard to the validity of opinion polls. By pointing out the great disparity between the two polls, he was able to cast doubt on the accuracy of opinion polls in general so as to discredit the privately conducted polls, while, at the same time, apparently accepting the Democratic party poll at its face value.

In another example, a confirmed bachelor used reasoning of this type subconsciously and in reverse, to avoid matrimony. He reasoned, on the one hand, that if a woman didn't care for him, there was little possibility of his marriage to her. On the other hand, if any woman *did* show an interest in him, she couldn't have very good taste, and he wouldn't be interested in any woman who was so lacking in discrimination. The result was that, in any case, he wouldn't get too deeply involved.

Although most examples of arguing in a circle are amusing and are often intended to be, this type of argument can often be used seriously, with more or less effective results. This is true, particularly, in the field of religion, where people are inclined to accept the traditional concepts without question. As a good example, there was an anti-evolution lecturer who stated in a public speech that no reputable scientist believed the theory of evolution. In the question-and-answer period which followed, someone in the audience said, "There is Dr. ___, a well-known biologist, who believes in the theory of evolution."

"Well," said the lecturer, "if he believes the theory of evolution, he's not a reputable scientist."

A similar possibility of being able to get an opponent either coming or going relates to the proposition that all things can be accomplished through faith. This is a proposition which cannot ever be positively disproved. If an exercise of faith achieves the desired result, you can always say, "See, it works"; but if it fails to bring fulfillment, you can say, "Well, you didn't have faith enough."

To be most effective, the technique of arguing in a circle should take on a quality of sophistication and complexity, so that the train of thought no longer moves in a single, simple circle, but along two or more interrelated circles in the form of a circle within a circle, or a figure 8. One of the most effective of these is the argument often used to prove the existence of God through the authority of the Bible. Arranged in the form of a series of questions and answers, this argument would be stated approximately as follows:

"How do we know there is a God?"

"The Bible says so."

"How do we know the Bible is true?"

"The Bible is the word of God."

"How do we know that the Bible is the word of God?"

"The Bible says so. Specifically, 2 Timothy 3:16 says, 'All scripture is given by inspiration of God.' Also, many of the writers of the Bible have recorded their actual conversations with God, and Jesus is recorded as referring to the Hebrew scriptures as the 'Word of God.' "

The final result is that, in a kind of indirect way we have completed an argument in a circle in which the Bible proves the existence of God, and God and the Bible together prove the truth of the Bible.

An even more elaborate and indirect argument in a circle can be used to establish the infallibility of the Pope. The question and answer dialogue for this argument would go about as follows:

"What is the basis for the theory of the

infallibility of the Pope?"

"He is God's representative on earth, and thus speaks with divine authority."

"How do we know that he is God's representative on earth?"

"The Bible records that Christ appointed St. Peter to be head of his church, and this position was passed on to the Popes as St. Peter's successors as head of the church in Rome."

"How do we know that this Biblical account is true?"

"The Pope has declared the Bible to be the Word of God, and therefore true."

"But how do we know that the Popes succeeded to St. Peter's position as head of the church?"

"Former Popes have interpreted Christ's commission to St. Peter as extending to them."

"But how do we know that this interpretation is correct?"

"As a pronouncement of God's representative on earth, this interpretation has the force of divine authority, and is thus correct."

While this type of argument can be seen to be obviously faulty when it is stated in dialogue form like this, it can be very effective in some situations and with certain audiences.

Generally the effectiveness of arguing in a circle rests on the fact that the whole argument is not stated all at one time, and that most people already accept one of the interrelated premises as true. Thus, where proper conditions exist, the skilled debater should be ready to use this type of argument, keeping in mind the rule that the relationships between interdependent premises should always be stated indirectly and at different times.

6
When Figures Lie

In entering upon a discussion of inductive logic, we come to the one type of argument which is widely regarded as fair and reasonable because it is based on observable facts rather than upon preconceived principles. Consequently, it is widely believed that there can be no argumentative tricks related to inductive logic, and that the only way to win an argument on this basis is to present more reliable facts than your opponent.

This popular conception, however, is not true. There is an old saying that "Figures don't lie, but liars figure," and this saying applies particularly to inductive logic. The final conclusion for any argument based on facts can vary greatly, depending upon the manner of selecting those facts and the way they are interpreted.

One of the commonest and most effective techniques for applying inductive logic to your advantage is the use of the "one-fact argument," which involves citing only one or a limited number of facts or incidents to prove a point, regardless of whether these facts are really typical of the argument to be proved. For example, you may find that a few birds have been killed by eating food that was sprayed by a certain insect spray, and use this finding to urge a total ban on the use of this spray; or you may experience unsatisfactory results from the use of a certain inexpensive house paint, and cite this experience to urge people to avoid *all* inexpensive paints, but to use the more expensive brand which you sell.

This technique is especially useful in connection with attacks against a government official or a government agency, because any government program, no matter how honestly and efficiently it is administered, is subject to human error, and you can almost always find at least one instance in which it seems, from outward appearances, that someone has fraudulently received some benefit to which he was not entitled or has been unfairly denied some benefit which was his due.

Having found one such example, you can play it up with constant repetition and lurid embellishments until people begin to think of this one example as typical of the total operation of the agency. In fact, in time you might begin to speak in general terms about the "corruption" or the "inefficiency" of the agency involved. This technique was used quite effectively by a radio commentator after World War II to hasten the elimination of price controls in this country by detailing, night after night for several weeks, the difficulties "three little Swiss guys" were having with the Office of Price Administration in their efforts to transform their small restaurant into a high-class one. This technique has also been used effectively in attacking public welfare agencies.

Of course, it is often difficult to get the information you need for such an attack on a government agency because the records of most agencies are confidential and unavailable to the average person. However, this may be an advantage rather than a handicap, because the confidentiality of the records makes them unavailable also to others who might want to check your story, and also prevents the agency from replying to your specific charges. You can get the information you need from the disgruntled claimant or the nosy neighbor, as the case might be, assured by the realization that you never need to be too definite in your charges, and, in most cases, need not even give the names of the persons involved.

A similar effect can often be obtained by stating a single general fact about social or economic conditions, without mentioning any extenuating circumstances or interacting social forces which may explain it. For example, you can always discount the achievements of an incumbent president of the United States by pointing out that he failed to stop a war, curb inflation, eliminate unemployment, or get the promised welfare bill enacted. Since no officeholder ever accomplishes all of his goals during his term of office, you can almost always cite one of these failures as a fact to be held against him.

Sometimes a one-fact argument is unable to stand alone to prove a point directly but can provide an *inference* that some other fact is true. For example, there is a strong implication of inefficiency in government operations in the statement that the government operated the railroads at a loss in World War I, or that the U.S. Post Office has traditionally operated at a loss, or that medical costs are rising in Great Britain where socialized medicine is in effect.

Likewise, you can imply the existence of work discrimination by using figures that show, in proportion to their total numbers in the labor force, there are fewer Negroes and fewer women in executive positions in industry than white men. Of course, there might be other explanations for these facts, and your opponent might point out that the purpose of the government's operation of the Post Office and of the railroads in World War I was not to make a *profit* in the ordinary business sense, that medical costs are rising everywhere, not merely in Great Britain, that Negro workers, on an average, do not have as much education as white workers, and that most women workers are generally not interested in work careers which would place them in competition with men for executive positions. However, you should not be concerned with bringing up these other possibilities yourself, because your opponent might not think to do so, and, even if he did, he would be at a disadvantage because you would have placed him on the defensive.

There is almost no limit to the inferences which can be drawn from one isolated fact. For instance, if people fail to appreciate one of your ideas and tell you it won't work, you can always point out that people did not believe Fulton either, when he made his steamboat. The implication is that since people were wrong about the steamboat, they could very well be wrong about your idea.

A similar argument is used in a drug advertisement on television. In this advertisement, there first appears a man in medieval garb, who makes the solemn pronouncement: "The world is flat." Then a man of the nineteenth century appears and says, "If men were intended to fly, they would have been made with wings." Finally, a woman comes on the screen and says, "All aspirin is alike."

The implication is clear. Having come to see that man's old ideas about the shape of the world and the possibility of flight are incorrect, people should understand that the old idea of all aspirin being alike is also false.

An extension of this idea is the familiar argument known technically as the *post hoc, ergo propter hoc* argument, which assumes that, "Since this happened after that, it is therefore the result of that."

You can assume a causal connection between

almost any two events which occur at approximately the same time, as has apparently happened in connection with our popular superstitions. For example, the belief that allowing a black cat to cross your path will bring you bad luck probably resulted from the fact that someone, sometime, experienced bad luck shortly after a black cat crossed his path.

The wide possibilities for finding causal relationships in isolated sets of facts is illustrated by the story of the scientist who trained a flea to jump at the sound of a bell. In order to find out what effect the flea's legs had in producing this response, the scientist removed one of the flea's legs after each jump until the flea had no legs left. Then, when the flea no longer jumped at the sound of the bell, the scientist concluded that removing the flea's legs caused it to go deaf. Other coincidences from which we may find a relationship of cause and effect are:

During the last two decades, DDT has been used as an insecticide, and in that same period there has been a sharp rise in hepatitis. Similarly, this rise in hepatitis has accompanied increased testing of nuclear weapons. It has also accompanied increased gasoline consumption and increased television viewing.

Sixty percent of all users of heroin started out using marijuana.

Sweden, which was one of the first nations to adopt a plan for socialized medicine, also has the world's highest suicide rate.

Calling attention to such coincidences can be especially effective in underrating the performance of an incumbent office-holder. All you need to do is to point out some undesirable social or economic condition which has come about during his term of office, and it is immaterial in most cases whether the adverse condition which is cited has any direct connection with the duties of the officeholder, or not.

For instance, you can downgrade the governor of your state by pointing out that crime has increased 20 percent since he took office, even though crime prevention is almost entirely the responsibility of local law enforcement agencies, and not of the governor. Similarly, you can make a good case for the election of a new president by calling attention to the immorality and lawlessness which is rampant in the country, or by citing the case of a man with a Ph.D. who is unable to find any but menial work under the present administration, and ignoring the fact that the president has only very indirect responsibility for the level of morality of the country, or for the ability of any individual to find suitable employment.

In similar fashion, you can often make an implication of corruption or indifference in government by connecting two widely separated incidents in the operation of a government agency. Examples of this are found in the following situations:

A corporation which has been indicted in a Federal court for violation of the U.S. anti-monopoly laws makes a large campaign contribution to the president's political party, and later, the monopoly charge is dismissed for lack of sufficient evidence.

Another corporation makes a generous contribution to the president's political party, and is later awarded a valuable bank charter by the government.

The federal agency charged with the responsibility for giving financial aid to school districts for the desegregation of the schools has dispensed only a small part of the billion and a half dollars appropriated for this purpose. The head of this agency is a southerner whose appointment was proposed by one of the President's political supporters in the south.

The director of the federal anti-poverty program shut down the projects for the poor in Minneapolis as an economy move at the same time that he bought new furniture for his office in Washington.

Similar parallels can often be used to associate an idea which you oppose with an idea or group which is generally disapproved of. Child Labor laws, public housing, or a reduction in our armed forces have often been denounced as "Communistic," simply by pointing out that they have been adopted by Communist countries or that they follow the Communist line.

A like parallel was illustrated in a recent cartoon in which a man with a gun, labeled "No gun regulation," was pictured beside a vulture, labeled "No atomic proliferation treaty," and the cartoon as a whole bore the caption, "Birds of a Feather." Other examples of such a correlation of ideas are found in the following statements:

Children today are not taught to work and be self-reliant, or to respect the rights and property of others, *but are willing to accept the benefits of the welfare state.*

People are not attending church any more, *and they are becoming socialistic in their thinking.*

The unwillingness of people to pass gun-control laws is astonishing, considering the recent assassination attempts. In fact, *it's comparable to the unwillingness of college officials to enforce the laws of their schools against people who destroy property and interfere with activities of law abiding students.*

A father must be boss in all relationships with the younger generation. We can't have the respect of our children by being buddies *or by getting drunk or exceeding the speed limit.*

There is growing atheism in this country *and an opposition to prayers in public schools.*

Pornography is based on a glorification of pleasure in the physical pain or humiliation of another. *This includes the glorification of war or any other violence against others.*

Of equal importance to the interpretation of facts is the determination of what the facts are in the first place. It has often been observed that different people observing the same event will differ greatly in their honest accounts of what happened. This gives wide possibilities to a skillful debater to find evidence for almost any fact he wishes to prove. This is illustrated by the account of a social study in which three skilled investigators of widely varied backgrounds were hired to interview a random sample of Skid Row derelicts to determine the causes of their conditions. One of these hired interviewers had been a temperance activist and crusader against the use of alcohol, one a dedicated Socialist and one a psychologist who had strong ideas about the effect of environment on people's lives.

As might have been expected, although each of the three interviewers tried honestly to record the causes which had led to the social situations of the men interviewed, the temperance activist found that the use of liquor had been a dominant factor in their downfall; the Socialist found the inequities of our economic system to be the dominant cause, and the psychologist found a close correlation between their childhood home environment and their present condition.

This same result can usually be accomplished by selecting the facts which tend to support your position, and ignoring those which do not. If you are a newspaper photographer or reporter covering an activist demonstration with which you are in sympathy, you might cover scenes in which the police manhandle the rioters but overlook scenes in which the rioters taunt and harrass the police or resist arrest.

Then, in interviewing a cross-section of the public afterward, you might possibly interview four of the rioters and one neutral bystander as a presentation of popular opinions regarding it. Similarly, if you oppose our participation in a foreign war, you can dwell on the terrors resulting from our bombing raids on enemy military targets, but ignore the terroristic activities and assassinations carried on by the other side.

Similar possibilities exist in regard to the use of statistics. It is not necessary to *alter* the figures you have, but it is always possible to *select* the figures that are more impressive. It is not very impressive to say that about two percent of heavy cigarette smokers get lung cancer, or that about five percent of all marijuana users eventually graduate to the use of heroin; but it *is* very impressive to turn those figures around and say the seventy percent of the victims of lung cancer were heavy smokers, and that sixty percent of all heroin users first used marijuana. Similarly, if you try to figure out the odds for any one individual ever to be involved in an auto accident in which his use, or failure to use, his seat belt would make a difference in his survival, you will come up with a very insignificant figure. But if you say that 10,000 people in this country lose their lives every year from failure to use seat belts, or that half of all auto fatalities could be prevented by proper use of seat belts, that can be very impressive.

In the presentation of an argument, you can often derive great advantage from the fact that most people have no access to the relevant evidence and no means of checking whether the facts are correct or not. This was brought home to me a few years ago when I was being instructed in the door-to-door selling of an encyclopedia. I listened to my instructor while he made a sales talk to a prospective buyer in which he gave many facts about the number of articles in this encyclopedia, the length of the articles, and the percentage of obscure and technical words in it as compared with another leading encyclopedia.

I asked him afterwards where I could get a brochure of these facts to use in my own sales talks. He said, "Hell, there's no brochure of those facts. But when you're making your pitch, you're in control of the situation. You can say whatever you want, and they won't be able to tell you different!"

On that basis, in almost any argument you can quote any facts which serve your purpose with the assurance that people will ordinarily not even think to question them. This can be especially true if you present the facts as being commonly accepted. Prefacing your statement with a comment such as,

"As you know," or "According to scientists," or "Historians tell us," will usually forestall any rebuttal. Otherwise, a bold, assured statement on your own authority will usually be sufficient. Who would ever be able to challenge statements like the following?

Five huge corporations with profits totaling 382 million dollars *paid no federal income taxes last year.*

There are many big insurance companies which *do not pay* any property taxes on their buildings, some of them as much as twenty stories high.

100,000 civilians were killed in Viet Nam as a result of our military action there, and one-fourth of these were children under twelve.

If proper action is not taken now to prevent it, water pollution will destroy all marine life in the Great Lakes in twenty years.

The "X" motor oil gives better protection to your car engine than other oil.

This unquestioning acceptance of stated facts is especially observable if the statement of fact is a printed statement or if it can be attributed to a statement which has been published. People tend to accept whatever they see in writing and cannot believe that anyone would make any statement in a newspaper or magazine article or in a book unless it were true.

As a final assurance that these stated "facts" will be accepted, it is important that they be given constant repetition. Hitler, in *Mein Kampf*, pointed out that you can get people to believe anything if you repeat it often enough, and that it is not even necessary that it be true. He asserted, in fact, that people will more readily believe a lie than the truth, and that the bigger the lie, the more readily it will be believed.

In making these repetitions, it is important that you ignore any challenges to your statements. If you oppose our country's participation in a foreign war, you can simply denounce it as an "immoral war." If someone asks in what way this war is immoral, or how it is more immoral than any other war, *ignore* the question, but upon the next opportunity, again denounce it as immoral. Eventually, the questioners will give up and quit asking their questions, and the other people, noting no further challenge to your statement, will conclude that it must be true.

A special type of inductive logic is involved in the use of forecasts and prophecies, for which a record of infallibility must be established to be effective. This record of infallibility can usually be established, however, from the fact that prophesies are typically stated in ambiguous terms, and can thus be interpreted to fit the facts of subsequent events.

This is illustrated by the familiar story of the consultation which Croesus had with the Oracle at

Delphi before his projected invasion of the Persian Empire, in which he was assured by the prophecy, "If you attack Persia, a great empire will fall." It was only after his disastrous defeat at the hands of the Persians that Croesus realized that the "great empire" whose fall was prophesied could have been identified as his own kingdom of Lydia.

Similar variations can be found in the interpretations for many of the prophesies in the Bible. The succession of Kings of the North and Kings of the South mentioned in the Book of Daniel have been variously identified with many different ancient and modern kingdoms, and "The Beast" mentioned in the Book of Revelations has also been variously identified.

In the first sermon I ever heard relating to the Beast in Revelations, it was convincingly described as representing Mussolini, then at the height of his power. The Mark of the Beast was identified as Mussolini's symbol, the fasces, which the speaker pointed out appeared on the reverse side of our own ten-cent piece. Since Mussolini's overthrow, I have heard the beast referred to with equal conviction as representing, among other things, World Communism, the Catholic church hierarchy, and the "liberal," nonfundamentalist Protestant churches.

Similar interpretations have served to establish the reputation of the medieval prophet Nostradamus. One of his obscure prophecies was the four-line stanza:

When the fork is supported by two pillars,
With six half-horns and six open scissors;
The very potent lord, heir to the toads,
Will then subjugate to himself the entire world.

These lines make absolutely no sense to most of us, but Henry James Foman, a modern expert on Nostradamus, has interpreted them in such a way as to present them as an uncanny prediction of a future event. Under his interpretation, the fork, representing the letter V, is sustained by two pillars to make an M, the Roman numberal for 1000. Six half-horns, represent CCCCCC, the numeral for 600, and the six open scissors are XXXXXX, the numeral for 60. In other words, the first two lines of the stanza represented the date 1660. Further, the toad was identified as the device of the Merovingian kings of France, of whom Louis XIV was the most prominent member, and it was pointed out that Louis XIV did become the dominant ruler of the civilized world in about 1660 as a result of his signing the Peace of the Pyrenees late in 1659, his marriage to Marie Theresa of Spain in 1660, and the death of Cardinal Mazarin in 1661.

In the same way, many of the modern prophecies have been established as true through a skillful interpretation. When Mrs. Jeanne Dixon, an astrologer, predicted in 1963 that Ivy League colleges would suffer a lessening in prestige, people saw no evidence that this prophecy would come true until her biographer, Ruth Montgomery, happily remembered that soon after this prophecy was made, Harvard-educated John Kennedy was replaced as president of the United States by Lyndon Johnson, who was a graduate of a little-known Texas college.

Similarly, when Edgar Cayce, a spiritualist, predicted in 1932 that a great catastrophe would occur in 1936, his biographer, Jesse Stearn, validated this prophecy by pointing out that 1936 was the year of the militarization of the Rhineland and the Italian invasion of Ethiopia (which had actually occurred the year before). To illustrate the possibilities for making favorable interpretations of such predictions, it can be shown that if Mr. Cayce had mentioned 1937 as the momentous year, it could have been pointed out that that was the year Japan invaded Manchuria; and if he had said 1938, it could have been explained that that was the year of the annexation of Austria and the Munich Conference.

Another aid in establishing the credibility of predictions is that in most cases they are based on an analysis of current events which makes them almost sure to come true. It does not take clairvoyant insight to prophesy, as the Bible does, that "there will be wars and rumors of wars" or to predict, as Edgar Cayce did in 1939, that there would be strife between capital and labor, or to forsee, as Jeanne Dixon did in the long period of the Cold War between the United States and Russia, that we would have trouble with Russia. Yet, while such predictions are not sensational, they do add to a prophet's score of correct forecasts and to his reputation.

In the event your prophet comes up with a prediction which is clearly incorrect and cannot be explained away, there are still some possibilities for minimizing the effect of it on his credibility. One of these is that people are generally not aware of all of a prophet's predictions, but only of the correct ones, and that you, in describing his success in predicting the future, would naturally mention only his correct predictions, making it appear that he was always right. Where one or two incorrect predictions do come to light, they may still not be particularly damaging to the seer's record of credibility, since people tend to forget or minimize incorrect forecasts and remember only the incredibly correct ones. As a last resort, the person making the prophecy or someone else on his behalf can always say that the signs were correct, but an error was made in reading them, as happened recently when a predicted earthquake for San Francisco failed to occur.

Such an explanation for an occasional incorrect prediction will usually be accepted, provided the credibility of the forecaster has already been established on the claim of his having access to information not available to ordinary mortals. It is important that people believe that he have such superhuman knowledge by having direct conversations with God, as Mohammed did, or by hearing voices, as Joan of Arc did, or by being visited by an angel in a dream, as

Joseph Smith was, or by having extrasensory perception, as the modern seers have.

By following these rules, presenting your selected authority as a person with a special insight which is denied to other people, interpreting his past predictions to fit later events, and ignoring or explaining away such of his predictions as may be found to be clearly incorrect, you can establish the credibility of almost anyone you choose to fill the role of a prophet, and then, on the basis of that credibility, use this person's further predictions to prove almost anything you may wish to prove about future events.

Better yet, with a little added showmanship and publicity, you might establish *yourself* as a prophet in your own right, and thus become your own authority for your predictions.

The ultimate in the use of inductive logic is to use a few examples to establish a general premise, and then to apply the general premise to similar specific instances. Plato used this technique convincingly in the dialogue *Charmides*, in which Socrates is recounted as using the examples of the advantages of quickness and speed in the activities of reading, writing, the playing of the lyre, and physical sports to prove that temperance, a recognized good, could not be a "slowness to act," as Charmides had first suggested. Other examples of generalities which can be made on the basis of a few observed examples are:

There are no atheists in fox holes.

Negroes are lazy.

All Communists advocate the violent over-throw of government.

The furniture was all badly scratched.

A similar type of generalization is the statement of facts in terms of *percentage* when no precise percentage figures are obtainable. For example, instead of merely saying that there has been a significant improvement or worsening in a situation, you can be more impressive by stating the facts in terms of percentages, as follows:

There has been a one hundred percent improvement in our operation.

Since employees have been making coffee in the office, cockroaches have increased one hundred percent.

The use of such generalizations is, of course, always risky. There is always a possibility that someone will know of one professed atheist in a fox hole, or one Negro who is not lazy, or one advocate of Communism who does not favor the use of force for bringing it about, or one piece of the furniture that was not scratched, or who, in response to your statement about the cockroaches, will ask, "What is the latest count?" However, the average listener will not possess the facts nor the analytical disposition to challenge your generalities, and the effectiveness of using them makes them worth the risk.

In this building up of generalities, it is often possible to take a few isolated instances which, of themselves, represent only minor injustices or errors in judgment, and to relate them together so as to present a picture of some great sinister conspiracy or concerted social wrong.

This was done a few years ago in connection with the great Communist scare, in which our concessions to Stalin at Malta and Teheran, our withdrawal of support from Chiang Kai-shek in his struggle against the Communists, and our unofficial support of Castro in his fight against the dictator Batista, were all cited as evidence of our own country's involvement in the Communist conspiracy to rule the world.

In more recent times, the government's plans to build a road in a scenic wilderness without consultations with the public, the rerouting of a freeway through a Negro community instead of an elite white neighborhood, the granting of oil leases on off-shore land without proper public hearings or safeguards against oil spills, and the refusal of the colleges and universities to grant an effective voice to the students in their administration and the selection of curriculums were all cited as evidence of our government's autocracy and its adherence to the interests of "the establishment." By thus associating various incidents together as parts of a general trend or development, it was possible to make each seem more sinister and more deserving of vigorous concerted opposition.

A similar strategy was used recently to link together the contemporary problems of rising prices and production shortages, and to ascribe them all to inefficiency, indifference, or corruption in the government. In the first place, it was possible to link the great rise in the cost of food to our government's recent sale of surplus wheat to Russia, which produced a shortage of feed grains in this country and thus raised the cost of feeding meat animals.

It was then pointed out that the present high cost of gasoline could be largely ascribed to the high excise tax levied on it, which accounted for almost half of its total retail price. Mention was then made of the lack of effective controls on farm prices and the lack of effective action against the creation of artificially produced shortages of petroleum products by the oil companies, to suggest that there was some dark conspiracy between the government and the producers of consumer goods, to keep prices high and to gouge the consuming public.

It is important to create an air of ugency about any subject you are debating by linking it with some great national danger. Hitler described this technique in his book, *Mein Kampf,* in which he pointed out that his campaign against the Jews was not based on any real opposition to them, but upon the fact that they could fit the role of a great public enemy against which he could unite the German people. This principle is based on the widely-observed fact that it is always more effective to oppose than to advocate, to attack than to defend, to "view with alarm" than to contemplate with hope, and to condemn than to praise.

In carrying out this principle, you can almost always identify any controversial question with some great national danger, such as the destruction of our environment, or the destruction of the people's rights and liberties. Thus, if you oppose the erection of a small industrial plant because of air pollution, point out the seriousness of air pollution on a national basis and its cost to the American people of six million dollars a year. If you find that the government has made a preliminary study for the possible erection of a dam which you oppose, report that the government has "secret plans" to erect the dam. If you oppose the government's plans for military spending, point out the ambitions of the military to dominate the government. If you oppose a tax ruling by the internal Revenue Service, describe the ruling as an attempt by the Internal Revenue Service to flim-flam the public.

This technique is especially effective if you can prophecy some dire consequences as a result of failure to accept your argument. It is always effective if you can tell your listeners that, if they do not agree with you, and do as you say, one of the following tragedies may occur:

They will suffer eternal torment in Hell.

They will unknowingly offend with their unpleasant breath or body odor.

The proposed activity will set off a chain of earthquakes, volcanoes, and tidal waves which will kill millions of our population.

Birds and other species of wildlife will become extinct.

The intellectuals will die out, and our society will degenerate to a level of mediocrity.

The entire human race will cease to exist.

The advantage of citing such dire predictions is that they involve conclusions which cannot easily be subjected to proof, and that even the experts on the subjects in question cannot say positively that you are wrong. You can point this out to any doubters by asking, "Can you be sure that this *won't* happen?" If they are logical, they will have to admit that we can never be absolutely sure of anything, and most of them will feel that they can't afford to take a chance on your being wrong. They will go along with your argument "just in case you might be right."

It is in this area of inductive logic that the proficiency of a skilled debater is most clearly demonstrated. Other argumentative techniques, i.e., begging the question or arguing in a circle, too often bear the marks of cheap trickery which expose them as unreasonable, but inductive logic bears the mark of unadorned truth which cannot be manipulated or explained away by any circuitous argument, or attacked by any means other than direct frontal assault.

The user of inductive logic thus moves out of the area of a clever debater into the greatness of an inspired crusader. That is not to say that inductive logic does not have its own required techniques. Basically, it is not a type of argument for the timid or the uncertain. It requires boldness, initiative, and unrestrained imagination. If you can acquire these qualities, your effectiveness as a debater can become almost unlimited.

7
Simplify! Simplify!

Having considered the various types of logic which can be used in an argument, it is appropriate to consider one of the general principles of logic which overrides and pervades all effective argument. This is the principle of *simplicity*, which reduces all arguments to their fundamental issues of right and wrong, good and evil, and black and white, and brushes aside the conflicting weighing of values which are wont to confuse the issues and interpose doubt and uncertainty in the path of clear-cut decisions.

This principle is illustrated by the story told about President Calvin Coolidge in connection with his attendance at a church service. Upon his return home from church, according to this story, his mother asked him what the sermon had been about.

"Sin," he replied.

"Well, what did the preacher say about it?" his mother asked.

"He said," replied Coolidge, "that he was against it."

This is the type of clear-cut simplicity which successful debating demands. In taking a position on any issue, always make sure to identify your stand as being unqualifiedly on the side of some recognized good, such as God, country, Motherhood, or the rights of the individual, and as being unalterably opposed to recognized evils such as Sin, Corruption, and high taxes.

In almost all arguments, if we analyze them objectively, we can see that both antagonists recognize the same basic values, but differ in regard to the relative importance of these values. You may find yourself in an argument over a proposed new program of assistance to the poor, which both you and your opponent agree would be socially desirable in relieving poverty and in stimulating the economy, but which would increase taxes, raise the national debt, and stimulate inflation.

Let us assume that you support the proposed measure because you feel that its humanitarian aspects and its possible effects in stimulating the economy outweigh the adverse effects of increased taxation and inflation. Your opponent opposes the measure because he feels the deadening effect of increased taxes and inflation on our economy would outweigh the benefits of the program. However, in carrying out the rule of simplicity, neither you nor your opponent should admit to the existence of these opposing considerations, because any such weighing of the pros and cons of an issue not only *weakens* your

argument, but makes the whole issue more compli-
cated and more difficult for the public to understand
or appreciate.

Instead, simply dwell upon the dire economic
conditions of the group which the legislation would
benefit, and, through this description of their needs,
imply that your opponent is not concerned with the
plight of the poor. In like manner, your opponent
should not try to expound upon the economic
principles involved, but should simply dwell upon the
burdensome effect of taxes and inflation on the
American people under present legislative programs,
and thus insinuate that *you* are not concerned about
the plight of American taxpayers, retired persons, or
others on fixed incomes who would suffer from
further inflation.

Similar principles might apply to a situation in
which you would be arguing in opposition to our
country's involvement in a foreign war in which we
have sought to help a small nation to protect itself
against attack by a neighboring nation.

You may be aware that persons who favor our
involvement in that conflict do so on the ground that
this will stop the spread of aggression by the nation
initiating the attack and help to build a World Order in
which all nations, including our own, will be free from
aggressive attacks in the future. However, in your
arguments in opposition to our participation in this
war, you should not give any recognition to the
reasons given by those who *favor* it, since this would

not only weaken your argument, but would also involve you in a discussion of issues which are complex, and thus uninteresting and difficult to understand. Instead, you should argue in terms which your listeners can easily understand and respond to, such as the senseless killing and maiming which takes place, the desolation of the countryside, and the resulting hordes of homeless and hungry people.

Thus, if the House of Representatives should fail to act on a Senate bill to end our participation in that conflict, you could comment that, "While our boys are dying in the war every day, the House Ways and Means Committee had bottled up the Senate amendment which would set a firm deadline for getting out."

Similarly, you could take note of the Supreme Court's recent decision banning capital punishment as "cruel and unusual punishment," to remark that, "If the life of a convicted murderer is worth saving, so much more is that of a draftee being sent to fight in an international conflict." Your opponents on this issue would likewise do well to shun the philosophical reasons for their position, and should direct their arguments chiefly to the issues which the people can feel and understand, such as the honor and prestige of our country and our duties to it.

Other possibilities for the use of the technique of simplicity can be found in the following imaginary situations:

You are arguing that the use of a certain insect spray should be banned because it has been found to be fatal to some birds, small animals, and beneficial insects, and to present a health hazard for human beings as well, while your opponent argues that in the absence of any other effective spray, the destruction of crops by insects presents a greater hazard to human life and health than does this spray.

You should ignore your opponent's comments about the threat which insects present to human life, and dwell instead on the destructiveness of the spray, elaborating on the number of birds, bees, and fish killed by it, and the number of rats which developed cancer as a result of being injected with it.

You are arguing over the question of prayers in public schools, and your opponent objects to them on the grounds that they violate the principle of religious freedom. Ignore this argument of your opponent and frame your own argument in such a way as to imply that he is simply an un-Christian person who is opposed to prayers in general. Emphasize this point by decrying the godlessness of the present generation and its dangerous drift from the teachings of the church.

You oppose your government's stand in branding Nation X an aggressor in that nation's attack on Nation Y. To make your argument effective, you should ignore the question of which nation was guilty of aggression, and assume that your government opposes Nation X because of prejudice against that nation or its leaders. You can bring out this point by saying that the people of the United States are sympathetic to the people of Nation X, even if the U.S. Government is not.

Your opponent opposes a bill to give the police more authority in detecting and arresting suspected criminals, believing that such a bill would deprive citizens of their constitutional rights. You should make no mention of the reason your opponent opposes this bill, but simply describe the alarming increase in crime and the diminishing safety of our homes and streets against crime and violence. Then, by mentioning that your opponent opposes this measure which would help to curb crime, you can make it appear that he is *not concerned about curbing crime.*

This technique of reducing an argument to its simplest terms can be especially effective where there is agreement regarding the ends being sought but a difference of opinion about the best method of bringing them about. Since a discussion of methods is usually dull and difficult to understand, you should ignore this question and concentrate on the purposes to be achieved. If you do this skillfully enough, you can make it appear that your opponent, in arguing against you, does not desire these results. The following examples will illustrate this technique:

You are arguing in favor of a proposed reorganization of a governmental agency which you believe would make its operations more efficient and thus save tax money, but your opponent argues that the proposed reorganization would not make for greater efficiency. You should ignore the basis of your opponent's argument, and instead dwell on the onerous burden of taxes on the American people and the vital need for relieving that burden through greater efficiency in government.

You are arguing in favor of a proposed new method of national defense which your opponent objects to partly because of the great cost involved, but chiefly because he believes it would not be effective. You should ignore the questions about the possible ineffectiveness of the plan, and concentrate your argument on whether we should risk our nation's safety for a paltry few million dollars in tax savings.

You favor a ban on the mail-order sale of firearms as a means of curbing political assassinations and other crimes. Your opponent argues that the mere prohibition of mail-order sales of firearms would not prevent criminals from getting guns, and would only serve to inconvenience law-abiding citizens in their purchase of firearms for hunting, target practice, or the protection of their homes. Disregard your opponent's argument about the ineffectiveness of the ban on mail-order sales, and insist that something be done to stop the vicious killings. Cite recent assassinations and attempts as evidence of the seriousness of the problem and thus make it appear that your opponent is obviously indifferent to crime.

In a discussion of the use of illegal drugs, your opponent argues that marijuana is not very harmful and that the penalty for its use should not be as severe as the penalties relating to other drugs. You maintain that the use of *all* illegal drugs should be strictly prohibited. To make your argument effective, ignore the fact that your opponent's comments relate only to marijuana, and then dwell at length upon the evils of the use of illegal drugs generally. As a final clincher to your argument, ask if he does not agree that we should put an end to the suffering and death which these drugs cause?

You are arguing that the use of military force is *never* justified, and that the world's problems can always be settled by peaceful political and economic means. Your opponent cites examples of nations which, lacking the power to resist, were overrun and subjugated by aggressive foreign powers. Do not try to make a responsive analysis of the situation cited by your opponent, but simply observe that a rich industrial society such as ours should be able to find alternatives to the violence of war, to use its great resources for building up instead of destroying, and to solve the urgent world problems of justice, freedom, opportunity, and economic well-being which now divide us.

You and your opponent are arguing about which is the true religion, and your opponent, in response to your insistence that yours is the only correct one, says that each man should have a right to the religion of his choice. This will give you an opportunity to say that it is not "our choice," but "God's choice" which we should try to find. By stressing this point, you can make it appear that your opponent had not been seriously trying to find the true religion, but instead has been trying to interpose his own preconceived ideas over the Word of God as set forth in the Bible in determining what that religion should be.

You are arguing for amnesty for army deserters and draft evaders on the ground that the war they refused to serve in was immoral and that they were thus acting on high moral principles. You are aware that the majority of the people of this country did not consider the war to be immoral, and that there is still a valid philosophical question as to whether anyone in a democracy has a moral right to set up his own judgment against that of the majority.

However, you should not become involved in a discussion of these complex philosophical issues, but should present the question as a simple one of morality versus immorality, and demand that the government grant amnesty to "all of the people who acted in defense of human rights and our Constitution."

You are arguing against the establishment of a national park on the ground that this would withdraw large tracts of timber from lumbering operations and thus have a depressive effect upon the economy of the area. Your opponent argues that the establishment of a national park would produce a sufficient increase in the tourist trade to overbalance the loss in the lumbering industry. You should ignore your opponent's argument about the effect of a national park on the tourist trade, and concentrate on what the losses would be in the lumbering industry in terms of jobs and lumber sales, and how important it is to maintain full employment in the area. By emphasizing this need for jobs, and by noting the nation-wide interest in the proposed park, you can make your opponent seem to represent the "outside interests," who are concerned only with a new "place to play," and not about the economy of the area.

Another way of simplifying an issue is to ignore the difference of opinion which caused another person or agency not to act on your suggestion, and to assume that this failure to act was merely the result of procrastination, inefficiency, or indifference. This is a technique which Harry Truman once used effectively when he dealt with the failure of Congress to pass the legislation he recommended by referring to that session of Congress as the "no-good, do-nothing 82nd Congress."

The following theoretical situations present other possibilities:

You have applied to a government agency for a benefit payment, but that agency finds that you are not entitled to the payment on the basis of the evidence you have submitted. While the agency is waiting for you to submit other evidence, you might have your attorney write to the head of the agency and to your representatives in Congress, complaining that the agency had had over three months to act on your simple claim, but had still *not taken any action.*

The government has been faced with the inter-related problems of unemployment, inflation, and increasing taxes, and has considered the possibility that any action taken to hold down taxes and inflation would perhaps *aggravate the unemployment situation*, while action to ease unemployment would perhaps bring about increased taxes and inflation. Finally, deciding that inflation is the more serious problem, the president takes action to curb inflation, with the hope that the unemployment problem might also be alleviated as the economy improves. This leaves the possibility that, if you later oppose the president's economic policies, you can ignore the hard choice he had to make between easing unemployment or inflation, and can say, "The president did nothing to eliminate unemployment."

You have participated in various demonstrations protesting against our participation in a war, or the curriculum offered by the college you attend, or the treatment being given to certain minority groups, but *no action has been taken by persons in authority to correct the situations you protested.* You should ignore the possibility that the persons you expected to act on your protests simply don't agree with you, and should protest that they "won't listen." You might ask, "How can we rely on conventional means of protest when we have a president who is unwilling to note the presence of a half-million citizens marching to protest his policies?"

You have alleged that law enforcement agencies in your area have discriminated against members of a certain minority group, and you supported your allegations by citing two examples of such apparent discrimination: one in which a man who killed a member of this minority group in a tavern brawl was never brought to trial, and one in which a law enforcement officer accused of using brutality in arresting a member of this minority group had never been disciplined. You are aware that the report of the sheriff's office regarding the bar-room slaying in question indicated that the killer had acted in self-defense, and that the district attorney's investigation of the alleged brutality by a law enforcement officer had indicated that no unnecessary force had been used in the arrest. However, you should ignore these announced findings of the sheriff's office and the district attorney, and should insist that something be done to rectify these injustices.

These principles have also been used successfully in advertising, where the sponsors of a product have stressed its one best feature to make it appear that this was the only important consideration. One recent successful display of this type was a television advertisement in which one ounce of a concentrated breakfast cereal was carefully measured out with the announcement that "This portion of the cereal would provide all of one's daily vitamin requirements." Then another cereal was carefully poured into sixteen one-ounce measures to illustrate that "It takes sixteen ounces of any of the leading cereals to equal the vitamin content" of the cereal being advertised.

Our immediate impression upon seeing this advertisement, the one which the advertisers no doubt wanted us to receive, is that the cereal in question is sixteen times more nourishing than any of the other "leading" cereals. However, this is not what the advertisers said. They said only that this cereal provided sixteen times more vitamins. They did not mention what other nourishment, if any, the cereal had, or how it might compare in total food value with the other cereals. The average television viewer does not take time to analyze or question such a statement.

Another similar example was a television advertisement featuring Dodge trucks, in which load capacity was treated as the only important consideration for buying a truck. This ad presented the information that a Ford truck of a certain model could haul 3800 pounds, that a comparable Chevrolet truck could haul 200 pounds more, but that the Dodge truck could haul 4800 pounds, "1000 pounds more than the Ford." The implication, clearly, was that the Dodge truck was much the better buy, but of course, that is not what the ad said. It merely said that the Dodge truck *would haul more,* and there was no comment about other features in which the Ford and Chevrolet trucks might be superior to the Dodge trucks. In fact, even in regard to load capacity, there are some pertinent questions which the ad sensibly left unanswered, such as:

In what way were the Ford, Chevrolet and Dodge trucks comparable? Were they of about the same weight? Or approximately the same price? Or what?

Why were the Ford and Chevrolet trucks unable to haul more than 3800 and 4000 pounds, respectively? Did they break down from the added weight if you tried to put bigger loads on them? Or were their engines unable to handle any heavier loads?

How was the load capacity of the three trucks determined? Was the load gradually increased on each truck until it finally broke down?

Ford and Chevrolet trucks are both made in various sizes. If a buyer wanted a truck with a larger load capacity than the models of the Ford and Chevrolet trucks in question, why wouldn't be simply buy one of a larger size?

By carefully stressing only load capacity, however, and by not offering any elaboration of their simple comparison, these advertisers for Dodge trucks were able to avoid having to answer these questions.

This technique of reducing an argument to its simplest terms is especially effective in connection with a negative argument, in opposition to a proposal for a new activity or change. This is because people are naturally reluctant to adopt any change, and readily accept any disparaging comment without elaboration. Thus, in order to "kill" an idea, you usually need only a simple statement such as the following:

That won't work.

We tried that once, but the people didn't like it.

It might work with a larger (or a smaller) group, but it wouldn't work for us.

We have the arrangements already set up.

We are not budgeted for it. It would cost too much.

We've always done it this way.

Our present way is working out all right, so why change it?

Let's not tamper with a good thing.

We did all right without it.

We're not ready for that.

It's against our policy.

Let's appoint a committee to study the question and report back to us.

Such a statement will put the originator of the proposal on the defensive and place the burden on him of explaining the complex details of his plan. Then you can raise objections to each detail until all agree that the plan is impractical.

8
Exercises in Frustration

Another good overriding principle for achieving success in argument is the use of a debating strategy which can frustrate your opponent in his efforts to come to grips with the question at issue, or to explain his position to you.

One of the most important techniques in this strategy is what I call the multi-prong attack, in which you diffuse and disorganize your opponent's argument by forcing him to deal with several issues at the same time. To accomplish this, you should continually disrupt his argument by challenging every statement he makes, whether it is pertinent to the argument or not. Then, before he has had an opportunity to answer one objection, raise another. Never give him a chance to complete an argument. If you cannot find anything else to raise an issue about, challenge his pronunciation of a word. This will not only divert his argument, but will make it possible, if you can finally prove that his pronunciation was wrong, to discredit him in regard to the main subject under discussion.

To find more to challenge in your opponent's argument, insist that he be definite about his proposals. Then you can find fault with their minor details. For example, if your opponent is arguing in favor of the government operation of a certain industry, you should ask him how he would have the managers of this business selected. He would have a choice of three possibilities. He could suggest that these managers be elected, or that they be appointed by higher officials, or that they be selected on the basis of civil service tests. In any case, no matter which of these three possibilities your opponent suggested, you then argue that this was not the way the managers of such a government business should be chosen, and, thus discredit the whole idea of his proposal.

At the same time, you should avoid being too definite or detailed in your own arguments. In criticizing the position of your opponent you should never propose an alternate plan. To do so would tend to put you on the defensive and place you at a disadvantage. This is because an attack on an idea is always more effective and draws more attention than the defense of an idea.

For example, if you are opposing the building of a dam on a certain river because of its possible effect on the ecology of the region, and your opponent argues that the dam is necesary to prevent recurring devastating floods on the river, dismiss his objections by a casual comment that some other method should be used to prevent the floods. Do *not* try to suggest what those other methods might be. Likewise, if you are arguing that the use of a certain insecticide should be banned in view of its possible harmful effect on animals or humans, and your opponent objects that such a prohibition would leave many of our crops unprotected against the devastating ravages of insects, you should suggest that *other means* be found for controlling the insects, but should not try to outline any specific methods which could be used.

This multi-prong attack need not be limited to interruptions of your opponent's argument. Your own argument can similarly be presented in a piecemeal fashion and be timed in such a way that he will be forced to deal with a *new charge* before he has had an opportunity to reply to the previous one. Let us suppose that you are arguing that the incumbent president of the United States had not lived up to his campaign promises. You should first mention that he had promised to end the war but had not done so. Then, before your opponent can point out that the president had taken all practical actions to end the war, you say that he had also not kept his promise about changing the welfare program. When your opponent tries to point out that the president needs the cooperation of Congress to make changes in welfare legislation, go back to the question of the president's war promises. Then, when your opponent finally gives up trying to answer your charges, suggest that he doesn't have an answer.

This technique can, in fact, become quite elaborate. Let us consider the possibilities of an argument that the present administration in the federal government is corrupt. You might start out by citing an instance in which a corporation was indicted in a federal court for monopolistic practices. The corporation then made a large contribution to the political party then in office, and the monopolistic charges were later dismissed. When your opponent tries to point out that there was not necessarily any connection between the political contribution and the dismissal of charges, you can point out that many contributions to the president's political party were never accounted for. Then, before your opponent can say that the unreported contributions were made *before* the law required them to be disclosed, bring up the report that one of the president's recent appointees illegally hired Mexican wetbacks. When your opponent tries to say that it had not been established that this appointee knew that the employees in question were Mexican wetbacks, and that, in any case, this did not prove that the whole administration was corrupt, you can return to the matter of the political contribution of the firm cited for monopolistic practices. By thus repeating these various charges without giving your opponent a chance to reply to any of them, you can eventually overwhelm him and build up a strong case for your argument in the minds of any outsiders listening in.

This device of putting your opponents on the defensive can be especially frustrating to them if you can charge them or their position with the same weaknesses which you anticipate *they* will charge against you. This was illustrated in the 1948 political campaign, when this country had a Democratic president and a Republican congress, and each political party blamed the other for the high cost of living. Such a charge against your opponents will not only give you the initiative, but will dispel opposing criticism, because people will not believe that you could be guilty of what you criticize in others.

Another good way to frustrate an opponent is to make a deliberate misinterpretation of a statement he has made, and then argue against what you have construed his statement to mean.

For example: If he says that the Marine Corps has received more than its fair share of the government's military budget, assume that he is saying that the Marine Corps is "no good," and take him to task for besmirching the good name of this military service.

Similarly, if your opponent makes a disparaging remark about student protesters who destroyed property or performed other illegal acts, interpret his statement as referring to *all* college students, and call to his attention the many serious, hard-working, and fair-minded students there are. Insist that *you believe* in today's young people, even if he does not!

If you are arguing against our country's military

action to help prevent a Communist government from imposing a Communist government on a neighboring country by force, and your opponent asks you if *you* are a Communist, ignore the logical import of his question and assume that your opponent is accusing you of being a Communist only because you disagree with him. Reply that "One should not assume that another person is a Communist only because he has different ideas."

If your opponent advocates a unified school system because he believes it can provide better education for the children, interpret his argument to mean that our parents and grandparents did not receive a good education in the one-room schools they attended. Show that this idea is wrong by describing all of the contributions which the older generations have made to our economy and culture.

If your opponent says that a certain small nation should not be forced by international pressures to take an insurgent group into its government without elections, but later says that this insurgent group should be represented in the international peace negotiations designed to settle that country's internal conflicts, maintain that he is now advocating the formation of an arbitrary coalition government such as he had previously rejected, and accuse him of an about-face on this issue to accept a point of view which you had advocated all along.

If your opponent argues that the property taxes in your area are unduly burdensome and should be partly replaced by an increase in the sales tax, assume that his argument is based on the premise that property taxes discriminate against the poor, and then point out that sales taxes also discriminate against the poor.

If a government spokesman denies that our government is "anti-Nation X" in the face of an international crisis involving the invasion of another country by Nation X, ignore the implications of this denial as merely a statement of long range policy, and assume that it means that our government supports Nation X in regard to that invasion. Then when our government officially opposes Nation X's action, insist that our government's spokesman lied and that our government is deceiving the people.

If your opponent argues for local rather than state control of natural resources, contending that "we don't want our resources managed for the benefit of outside interests," assume that the term, "outside interests," relates to tourists, rather than to outside land subdividers and developers, and then argue that we *need* tourists to boost our economy!

If a military officer says that long hair on men "carries connotations of laziness, inattention to details, recalcitrance, or lack of pride," ignore the fact that this statement applies to our present styles and customs, and interpret it as applying to the wearing of long hair *per se.* Then point out that most of the great men in our country's early history wore their hair long.

Pretend that the proponents of the theory of evolution believe in our direct descent from apes. Then you can announce a public debate on this issue by saying, "Do you believe your grandfather was an ape? If you do, come prepared to defend your family tree at the ___ church tonight."

If your opponent makes a statement that society should provide "meaningful and dignified employment for all," interpret this statement to mean that your opponent would have the government set up an agency to see that everybody had a job which met these requirements. You can then cite the ridiculous instance in which a worker would go to this agency and ask for a new job because his present one "wasn't dignified enough."

If your opponent argues that goods could be sold to the people cheaper under socialism than under capitalism because the government would not have to make a profit, interpret this to mean that the government would not have any source of income, and ask how the government could operate at all without an income.

If your opponent says he believes Negroes should have social equality with whites, imply that he is advocating the *intermarriage* of Negroes and whites, and ask whether he would like to have his sister marry a Negro.

If your opponent says that hard-working, responsible people should not be taxed to support the lazy and improvident, interpret this to mean that the more fortunate should not be punished to support the less fortunate. Then assert that you do not feel punished in being able to support the government which has done so much for you and enabled you to gain the wealth you have.

If a candidate for public office says that he has been brainwashed about some important issue as an obvious means of indicating that he had been misinformed on the subject, interpret this as an admission that he is easily misled, and argue that this is evidence that he is unqualified for public office.

A similar argumentative technique is the use of what I call the Bogey Man or Straw Man argument, in which you present an argument for your opponent which is easy to refute and then proceed to refute it. For example, you may be arguing against our participation in a war which your opponent supports on the ground of national security or the maintenance of world order. You should ignore the reasons given by your opponent, and assign some base motive to our participation in the war, such as the maintenance of full employment in this country, or the preservation of our honor and prestige, or the need to save face for our country or our president.

Then you can devastatingly dispose of these assigned motives by stating, "There is something very wrong with our country if we have to depend on war to keep our economy up," or, "We are killing hundreds of people in order to save face for one person," or "For the United States to hope to gain anything in world prestige by beating a little country like that is ridiculous."

A similar technique could be used for defending the truth of the Bible. If your opponent expresses doubts about parts of the Bible, it is probable that the account of the miracles is what he doubts. However, do not try to prove the truth of these miracles, but establish the general truth of the Bible by showing that other expressed doubts about it had been unfounded.

You could say that people had doubted that Ur could have had a civilization sufficiently advanced to produce a man like Abraham, but that recent research has shown that Ur had, in fact, a very high civilization, and a knowledge of writing. Likewise, you could point out that many people have doubted St. Luke's account of the life of Jesus, but that in fact,

St. Luke has been found to be accurate in his narration of historical events.

Other possibilities for the use of the Bogey-Man argument are shown in the following examples:

A proposal has been made to reduce property taxes because they are unduly burdensome and unrelated to the individual's ability to pay, with the resulting loss in revenue to be made up by increases in other taxes. In opposing this proposal, you should charge its proponents with claiming that it would lower taxes in general, and then point out that this is not true, but that in fact the proposal would cause *increases* in income and sales taxes. If you stress the increases in sales and income taxes enough, you could even make it appear that the proposal would bring about a *total increase* in taxes.

Your opponent is arguing for a liberalization of our abortion laws. Instead of arguing the merits or disadvantages of his proposal, simply elaborate on the point that there is no constitutional right to have abortions.

There is a bill before Congress to withhold funds for a military operation overseas at a time when the president is trying to negotiate a settlement of the conflict involved, and it is being argued by those who oppose this congressional action that it is ill-timed and would hamper the president in his negotiations. In supporting the proposed bill in Congress, you should avoid any discussion of its advisability or inadvisability, but should concentrate on the fact that Congress has a *right* to take such action.

You are opposing the government's farm program under which the government buys up surplus farm produce in order to keep it off the market and sustain farm prices. You should ignore the purpose of this program and simply argue against it on the grounds that we *do not need* a reserve of farm produce for future use.

In advertising a certain brand of cigarettes, you should not risk being placed on the defensive by making positive statements about its good qualities, but should imply that other cigarette manufacturers had made *unfounded* claims about theirs. Then refute those imaginary claims by asserting that "No medical evidence, or scientific endorsement, has proved any other cigarette to be superior" to your brand.

You oppose the establishment of a proposed national park, but do not have a convincing reason for doing so. Pretend that the issue involved is the sum that would be reimbursed to owners of the land to be used for the park, and assert that you would not favor the park unless the private owners of the lands are fully and fairly paid for them. This will put you on the side of the opponents of the park and place its proponents further on the defensive without your making any statement which anyone can argue with.

A similar result can be obtained by defining some of the terms used by your opponent to mean something different from what he obviously intended, and then pointing out how ridiculous his statement is as you have defined the terms.

For example, if your opponent states that most poeple marry for love, you can prove him wrong by ignoring the traditional meaning of "love" as it applies to relationships between men and women, and defining it instead, in St. Paul's terms, as a feeling which "Beareth all things, believeth all things, hopeth all things, endureth all things." Since few married couples experience such selfless devotion to each other, it will be evident that your opponent's statement is not true.

A like possibility can apply to the word, "liberal," as it relates to political or economic ideas. Assume that you are in a discussion about a political candidate whom your opponent apparently favors but you oppose, and whom your opponent refers to as a liberal, meaning a person who advocates political and social changes in the interests of the common man. Realizing that the term "liberal" has great popular appeal, you can show that this label should not apply to the candidate in question by saying that a liberal is a person who champions the rights and liberties of the individual as opposed to the government. By using this definition, you will not only be able to prove that the term does not apply to this candidate, but you will also probably leave your opponent confused as to what label he can use to describe the candidate's political leanings.

This use of special definitions can also be effective in arguments involving religion. If your opponent says that he does not believe in the existence of God, you can point out that God is simply the composite of all that is good, such as the forces of evolution, the beauties of nature, or the feelings of love and devotion which people feel for each other. You might even quote some of the closing lines of W.H. Carruth's poem, "Each in His Own Tongue" to say, "Some call it Evolution, but others call it God," or "Some call it Consecration, but others call it God." Ask your opponent if he does not believe in evolution, and devotion, and the beauties of nature. Since he must agree that he *does* believe in these things, he must yield and agree that he does believe in God.

Another good way to frustrate your opponent is to belittle his position by contrasting it with more important things he should be concerned about. For example, if your opponent is speaking favorably of our president's activities in the field of foreign affairs, you can always bring the situation into proper perspective by a comment such as, "The president is more concerned with keeping President Thieu in office in Vietnam than in getting our prisoners of war back," or "The president has time to go to China, but not to go to Harlem to study the social and economic problems there," or "He has time to talk to Chou En Lai, but not to the poverty-stricken people of Appalachia." This technique could also apply to the following situations:

You oppose the government's new space project, which is to be partly devoted to a study of the effect of weightlessness on the human body. You might point out that no one has yet died from weightlessness, and the money might thus be better spent on a study of ailments which people do die of, such as heart disease.

You are defending the theft of secret government records which were released for publication, as a means of opposing the nation's war effort. You can justify the theft by asking, "Is it more important to keep secrets or to *stop the killing in the war?*"

You oppose a proposed government subsidy to an airplane manufacturer to build a supersonic plane which would help this country to maintain its leadership in passenger air travel. At the same time, you note that there has been a reduction in the government's school lunch program. You can mark the baseness of the proposed airplane subsidy by suggesting that the government, by depriving hungry children of school lunch money, can save enough money to bail out the inept executives of the airplane factory.

You oppose some proposed changes in welfare regulations which would remove about fifty employable persons from the county welfare rolls and result in a saving to the county of $10,000 a month, or about $120,000 a year. You can point out that the county residents pay at least $18,000 a month or $216,000 a year in the government's excise tax on telephone service, which is used to help finance our country's military operations abroad, and you can then say, "That's $216,000 *for death*, and only $120,000 *for life*. Can we really afford to make welfare the scapegoat, while we spend billions for destruction?"

A variation on this technique is to give figures showing the small amount of time or money we have been devoting to a recommended activity in comparison with other, less desirable activities. For example, if you want to shame your listeners into devoting more time to education or religion, you can quote the following figures for the amount of time the average person has spent in various activities up to the age of 70:

Eight years in amusement
Six years in eating
Eleven years in working

Twenty-four years in sleeping
Five and one-half years in washing and shaving
Six years in walking
Three years in conversation
Three years in reading
Three years in education
Six months in worshiping God.

In like manner, a plea for a greater expenditure of funds for the support of one's church, welfare, or charity can always be made more effective by a comparison of amounts being spent for these purposes with amounts being spent for less worthy purposes, such as war, liquor, gambling, or movies. You can make a more effective appeal for more cancer research by our government by mentioning that in 1969 for every man, woman, and child in this country, our government spent:

$125 for war and preparation for war
$19 for the space program
$19 for foreign aid
89 cents for cancer research

Similarly, to persuade people to give more to their church, you can point out that the average American family now spends about $622 each year, or about 6.3 percent of its income, for recreation, but only about $138, or 1.4 percent of its income, for religious and welfare purposes.

The final and ultimate means of frustrating your opponent is to change the subject before he has had a chance to develop his argument. This not only disconcerts and exasperates him, but it also serves to divert the argument to a subject which you can discuss with greater advantage, or in which you have more popular support. This will put your opponent in the position of either agreeing with you on the new subject, (which will make him seem to concede that you were right all along) or of trying to continue his original argument which will make him seem to take an unreasonable position in regard to the new subject.

This technique requires the development of a certain finesse, but it can be easily applied in any family situation where a discussion of personalities is involved. For example, if your opponent mentions a member of your side of the family, you can bring up something undesirable about his side of the family, and thus divert the argument to a discussion of *his* family background.

In a similar fashion, if your opponent criticizes you for something you have done, or the way you have done it, you can usually think of something that he or the group he is supporting has done wrong, and can call this to his attention as a means of diverting the argument. For example:

If your father argues that your practice of shifting the family car to a lower gear as a means of

slowing it down for curves is hard on the transmission, you can counter by saying that this is no
harder on the transmission than *his* practice of leaving
the car in overdrive for city travel.

If you are defending an activist group which has
been accused of various criminal activities including
arson, you can put their accusers on the defensive by
saying, "When you talk about arson, you should
remember that Hiroshima was a pretty good example,
and *that* was an act of the United States Government."
For a still broader defense of this group, you could
say, "This group has been called our number one
problem. That's ridiculous. They didn't cause Vietnam, widespread hunger, unemployment, pollution,
or the other serious social problems that plague us."

If you are attacking the president's foreign
policies and your opponent suggests that you wait and
see how those policies work out, you can say that you
cannot take a "wait and see" attitude as long as federal
troops are killing peacefully demonstrating college
students as they did at Kent State University.

If you are arguing against the Supreme Court's
ruling banning prayers in the public schools, you can
note the fact that the court, at about the same time,
asserted the right of homosexuals to receive maga-
zines in the mail relating to their common interests.
Then you can divert the argument to a discussion of
homosexuals, and make your opponent seem to be

defending them, by saying, "If something is wrong, it is wrong with the Supreme Court.' The upshot will seem to be, 'Obscenity, yes; prayers, no.' "

Another good way to change the subject is to suggest to your opponent that he would probably take a certain stand on a similar, related subject, based on his stand on the subject under discussion. This is especially effective if he has taken an extreme position on the question at issue and you can goad him into an even more extreme and untenable position. If your opponent is arguing in favor of a high minimum wage for all workers, you can say, "And I suppose you'd say we should pay them all public assistance benefits when they are not working." Likewise, if he is arguing that labor unions have a just reason for trying to maintain union shops, you can say, "And I suppose you would say the unions should have a voice in deciding who should be hired for work." Such a comment should serve to divert the discussion to a subject with which you can deal more comfortably, or, at the least, should permit you to break off the argument gracefully and without losing face.

Sometimes the subject of the argument will suggest parallels with other subjects which can be referred to as a means of changing the subject. Let us suppose that you are arguing that the use of DDT should not have been banned because the menace of insects in destroying food for starving millions is a greater menace to mankind than DDT. You can reinforce your argument and also direct it toward a more easily defended position by pointing out that there was a similar folly in the government's banning of cyclamates in no-calorie food sweeteners in the face of the greater health hazards of obesity, and in its warnings against the use of "the pill" as a contraceptive in the face of the greater dangers of pregnancy and over-population.

As a last resort, you can always introduce a new subject by mentioning it at the end of a summary of charges you have already made in the course of your argument. For example, if you have been arguing that the present administration in Washington has done a poor job of meeting our country's economic problems, you can sum up by saying, "Under this administration, we have had the highest cost of living we have ever had, the most unemployment, the greatest crime rate, and the most traffic congestion."

Then, before your opponent can recover from his surprise at the mention of traffic congestion, or try to answer your charges about the cost of living or unemployment, you can outline a proposal for the allocation of federal funds to develop rapid transit systems for our large cities. By the time you have gotten into this subject, which no one would argue about, your opponent will probably decide that the original subject is not worth trying to revive, and he will let you complete your learned discussion of traffic problems without interruption.

It is not necessary, as in this case, that the list of charges or complaints which leads to the new subject be related to the original question under discussion. It is enough that, in arguing on either side of almost any subject, you will have occasion to view some act or idea with alarm, and that will give you the opportunity to decry the entire state of our civilization with some remark as, "This country is just not what it used to be."

Then you can proceed to mention all the things that are wrong with the country, ending with a statement on some safe, noncontroversial subject such as law and order, civil rights, or the destruction of our environment. You might say, "Things are certainly not the way they used to be. In the old days, people used to figure on working hard and being independent, but now the kids don't want to work, and they seem content to live off welfare. Crime is rampant on our streets, the kids are all using drugs, and we are destroying our environment with our heedless pollution of our land, and air, and water."

There! You have safely arrived at the subject of land, air, and water pollution, about which everyone agrees something must be done. The secret of this technique for changing the subject is to move right along, once you have started listing the undesirable features of our society, without any pause for your opponent to intervene until you have reached the noncontroversial subject. Then he will not consider it worthwhile to intervene, and his silence from that point on will make you seem to be the winner of the argument and will leave you free to present the new subject as an authority of outstanding discernment and wisdom.

Another very effective method of changing the subject is the technique of giving an *unresponsive* reply to questions put to you on the problems at issue. This not only serves to divert the discussion into new channels, but can help you to avoid having to give damaging or embarrassing answers, or being pinned down to take a definite stand. Let us assume that as a candidate for a public office you have been accused of having a secret campaign slush fund for which you have not properly accounted and which was contributed by individuals to whom you will be politically indebted. In answering these charges, you should not try to explain the origin or nature of this fund or state whether you were under any political obligations to the contributors, but should instead tell about what a hard time you and your wife had and how you worked your way through college. You should also talk about your little dog (if you have one), and should mention that your wife is Irish (if she is). This should convince people that you are really a very fine person, and that your accusers are only trying to make trouble for you.

Following are other examples of the effective use of nonresponsive answers as a means of turning the course of an argument and avoiding the impact of embarrassing questions:

Question: Don't you agree that the ___ is a sturdy, durable automobile?

Answer: I think it rides like a lumber wagon.

Question: Don't you think Rev. ___ had a great message in his sermon?

Answer: I think he's insincere.

Statement: I think the woman was just as much to blame as the man was.

Reply: I disagree. I think the man was just as much to blame as the woman was.

Question: How do you stand on the question of school busing?

Answer: I am not for busing or against busing, but for quality education. I do not believe our school children should become political footballs.

Question: What do you think about the proposed changes in the Social Security Act?

Answer: I have always supported the interests of our elder citizens, and I think they are deserving of the best that we can give them. I think that one of the most important things we can do to advance their interests is to maintain a vigorous, expanding economy which will enable all working people to provide for a comfortable old age. We should then control inflation, so that these savings for old age will not become dissipated. These are the types of economic programs I have supported, and will continue to support, in the halls of Congress.

The techniques outlined in this chapter are principally of a defensive nature, and therefore not the type of technique to be included in your normal bag of argumentative tricks, since successful debating depends primarily on *maintaining the initiative*.

Nevertheless, there will be times when these techniques will be useful, when you will have encountered a debater who is even more skillful than you are, or who, by some means, has hit upon a telling argument which you cannot refute, but can only hope to soften through some evasive tactics. Then, you should be prepared to use these techniques, hoping that, though you can no longer *win* the argument, you might at least avoid obvious defeat.

9
The Use of Force

At first glance, a chapter on the use of force in regard to the art of argument might seem out of place in this enlightened age of democratic governments and trials by jury. However, it is a fact that many arguments are still settled by force, as is illustrated by the prevalent practice of settling disputes by invitations to "come outside and say that." Moreover, force is still used in many other, subtle ways to settle arguments involving economic, political, or social pressures, rather than physical power. This is illustrated by the familiar story of the efforts of an industrial firm to establish a company-sponsored union for its employees.

According to this story, there was one employee whose refusal to join the company union jeopardized the whole union plan. The president of the company finally called the man in to talk to him about it.

Facing the recalcitrant employee, the president said, "This company has gone to great pains to build up pleasant working relationships with its employees and to provide a union through which the employees can express their desires. But of course, if anyone doesn't wish to work in that kind of relationship, he might be happier to look for work elsewhere."

Under this implied threat, the employee quickly agreed to join the union. Later, when asked why he had changed his mind about it, he said, "Well, I had never had it explained to me so well before."

Another pertinent story regarding the attributes of force in our modern society involves a young Indian boy who was asked by a friend to lend him his rope. Not wishing to lend the rope, the Indian boy said that he could not because he needed it to tie his blanket. Later, one of his friends said to him, "What do you mean, tie your blanket? How would you tie it, and why?"

He replied, "If one does not wish to lend his rope, any reason will do."

The point of both of these stories is that if you have the economic, political, or social power to have your way about anything, you do not need a logical reason for it. In fact, any reason at all is usually irrelevant.

This was impressed upon me several years ago, at a service club luncheon meeting in a small town in the Rocky Mountains. An announcement was made that the U.S. Forest Service had ordered a cutback in the number of cattle which could be grazed in the national forests, based on this agency's findings that the forests were being overgrazed. Realizing that they were all dependent on the cattle ranchers in the surrounding area for their own economic prosperity, the members of this service club quickly proposed and passed a motion to send telegrams to their representatives in Congress, protesting this action by the Forest Service, and declaring that they believed the forest lands would continue to provide pasture at the current level.

I remember turning to some of the men sitting near me during the discussion of this motion and asking, "How many head of cattle will the forest lands support?", but the only reply I received was a sheepish grin from a fellow sitting across the table from me. There was not one person at that meeting who had been trained in the science of forestry or land management, and there was not one, in any case, who had examined the forest lands in question to see whether they had indeed been overgrazed or not. Nevertheless, they sent their telegrams to members of Congress, and those telegrams, together with other similar telegrams from other service clubs in the area, had an influence in modifying the government's directives regarding grazing rights.

This is a result which can be accomplished by any organized group action, whether this action is expressed in the form of a petition to Congress, in the form of a boycott, a picket line, a public demonstration, the consensus of a mob, or the simple democratic process of electing our lawmakers.

By the mere weight of numbers, and without the presentation of any evidence whatever, such a group can settle the question of how many head of cattle can be grazed on public lands, or who is right in an industrial dispute, or whether the erection of a high-rise hotel at a certain location will harm the ecology of the area, or whether the theory of evolution is true.

To achieve this result, it is not necessary that the group in question represent the majority view of the population in general, for the whole idea of an activist group is that it can wield an influence out of proportion to its numbers. This influence is largely due to the fact that any group demonstration or activity, even though it may be peaceful and non-violent in its mode of operation, constitutes a menace to the safety, the well-being, or the peace of mind of other people.

In a literal sense, there can be no such thing as a peaceful demonstration. At best, they all present what the late Martin Luther King termed a "confrontation," and that involves at least an emotional unpleasantness. Moreover, any demonstration involves some element of physical force, such as the mere occupation of a street, sidewalk, or public building by a group of demonstrators which presents a physical barrier to the access to these areas. Add to this the fact that any mass demonstration can get out of hand and *lead* to violence, and you have a situation so menacing to the public peace and tranquility that many people will be willing to yield to the demands of the demonstrators at almost any cost, rather than face the prospect of the further unpleasantness which continuing demonstrations might bring.

The effectiveness of a demonstration is further shown by the fact that it can present a level of more popular support than it really has. This is because the public can see and hear the 10,000 people of a minority group who are engaged in the demonstration, but cannot see or hear, or even, in many cases, know of the existence of the 1,000,000 people of the silent majority who have remained at home. This impression can be further developed through a carefully planned combination of violence and propaganda. The use of violence, or the threat of it, will shock the public into reexamining its position on the question, will bring support from liberal groups who would not, themselves, condone such violence, and will encourage repressive action by law enforcement agencies, which will help to prove the activists' contention that the "establishment" is repressive of new thought. In any event, the propaganda effects of a demonstration tend to mushroom. Because a demonstration is exciting, it receives a great deal of publicity, and this adds to the repetition of the demonstrators' propaganda and gives further force to the impression that they represent the majority view. The result is that if the people with opposing views do not come forward with counteracting arguments, the public will gradually come to accept the viewpoint of the activists. This results from the fact that the majority of the people really do not have any strong feelings or opinions about the great controversial issues but are inclined to go along with whatever seems to be the prevailing views. These same principles apply to the settlement of issues at public meetings. It is an observed fact that the vast majority of people in attendance at almost any meeting are largely undecided about any of the questions before the group, and will routinely approve almost any proposal that is made. It is very important, therefore, if you feel strongly about some controversial question which is to be decided at such a meeting, that you try to arrange to have the vote taken on that question at a time when your faction can *take the initiative*, and submit the motion to be voted on.

For example, if your organization is planning to decide on the details of your annual picnic and you prefer to have it at the lake where you can go swimming, but you know that there is a small faction in the club that wants to have it at a recreational pavilion where they can dance, you should arrange to have a couple of people at the meeting who will promptly make and second a motion to have the picnic at the lake. If you can do so, the organization will almost certainly decide to have the picnic at the lake, because the ten percent of the group who favor the lake, plus the sixty percent who hadn't really thought about it before will carry the motion overwhelmingly.

On the other hand, if the opposing faction should out-maneuver you and present their motion before you can present yours, you should move to have their motion tabled until you can study the question further. This will give you an opportunity to work on the neutral members of the group before the vote is taken, and perhaps even give you an opportunity to regain the initiative at the future meeting.

These same variations in the use of force can also apply in arguments between individuals. We have already noted the use of fisticuffs as a still familiar method of using force in settling individual disputes. However, this type of force need not be based on a formal invitation to step outside, but might merely consist of a loud and angry approach to the question at issue. If your opponent is a timid, retiring person, this can be very effective.

Economic force in individual arguments can take the form of a refusal to do business with the other person if he fails to agree with you. A similar use of force is to withhold affection from a spouse or loved one if he does not accept your viewpoint. In other situations, this force might take the form of social pressure, in which you overwhelm the other person with the popularity of your viewpoint and make him feel isolated and out of tune with the popular consensus. This can be done by challenging him to "put up or shut up" with some such statement as, "Do you want to bet on it?" or "Put your money where your mouth is," or "You will find that the voters don't agree with you," or "Your candidate doesn't have a chance."

A similar "put up or shut up" strategy is to

challenge your opponent to equal or surpass the accomplishments of someone whose work he is disparaging. If he is criticizing the acts of your city's mayor, ask him if he can do better; or if he denies that the Bible is of divine origin, challenge him to write a parable having the literary excellence of those in the Bible.

As a final technique in the use of force and as a last resort, you can always lose your temper. I call this a last resort because a loss of temper is always a subtle, unspoken indication to your opponent that you have no other argument to offer him, and that he has, in effect, won the argument. However, it is always better to give this tacit admission of defeat by losing your temper than to acknowledge expressly that you were wrong. Besides, by losing your temper, you can at least have your way about the matter in question. This strategy is particularly effective if you are arguing with a close friend or a member of your family, who would be hurt and unhappy to have you angry with him.

Another argumentative technique similar to the use of force is the argument that your opponent's position is dangerous, dishonorable, immoral, unwise, or unpleasant to contemplate, and that he should change his opinion on the question at issue, because it would be to his advantage, or the advantage of mankind generally, for him to do so. These arguments are usually based on one of the following general premises:

That the other person can avoid some dire consequence, or bring about an end to some intolerable situation, by accepting your point of view.

One illustration of this type of argument is that a person should accept certain religious beliefs in order to avoid the agonies of Hell or assure himself of the joys of Heaven.

Another illustration is the argument that we should sign a treaty with an enemy country in order to get our prisoners of war back, even though the terms offered by the enemy were admittedly unjust and dishonorable.

That it is good for the individual, or for society, that people believe certain things.

This premise is illustrated by the arguments that people should believe in a life after death, because this idea gives them happiness and peace of mind, and that they should believe in Hell because otherwise they will not live good, virtuous lives.

That the other person should give up his ideas in order to bring greater unity among the parties concerned.

Arguments of this type might be in the form of an appeal to a rival faction of a political party to give up its adverse stand in order to present a united front in the forthcoming election, or an appeal to a rival political party to refrain from criticism of the administration's foreign policies, in order not to weaken the government's bargaining power in its negotiations with other countries; or a request that an opposing block in the state legislature give up its opposition to a pending piece of legislation in order to end the current deadlock and allow other urgent legislation to be passed; or a complaint about the disruptive divisions among the Christian churches and a plea to the people of other Christian denominations to end this disunity by joining *your* denomination. (Of course, you would not want to give up *your own* political or religious affiliations to achieve such unity).

That certain ideas are socially unpopular, and any person who holds them should give them up in order to have greater social acceptance and further his chances for economic or political advancement.

Illustrations of arguments based on this premise are: "If I were a Socialist, I would never admit it," or "Who wants to believe that he descended from monkeys?" or "You'll have to change your religion if you want to work in that Mormon Community."

That we should do what the other fellow wants us to do, because he is "a good guy," or is "deserving."

This premise is illustrated by the arguments that one should vote for a certain candidate because he is a "good Christian" and is good to his family, or that we should not sign a certain treaty with a nation which had been unfriendly with us in the past, because it might have an adverse effect on our relations with other countries which had been our friends for years, or that a man who had been found to be ineligible for welfare benefits should receive them anyway, because he "had paid taxes all these years, was a good loyal American, and was just as much in need as many others who were receiving benefits."

It is true that the use of force for settling arguments is no longer as important as it once was. Gone is the institution of trial by combat, and gone also are the Inquisition, the rack, and the stake. Yet, as we have seen, there are still occasions when the use or threat of force, or an appeal to expediency, can be decisive in settling controversial issues.

Where such arguments can be used, they offer much to commend them to the serious student of argumentative practices. Basically, they appeal to the mature debater because they are simple and decisive. *They either work or they do not.* There is never any doubt about the outcome. Also, in any argument based on force or a consideration of the other person's own self-interest, one troublesome question regarding the major premise of the argument becomes no longer pertinent and needs no longer to be considered.

That is the question of whether the premise is true.

10
The Appeal to Reason

There is one final technique for effective argument which will have occasional application, and which should be considered. That is the use of what is popularly known as reason. There will be rare occasions in which you will have private information regarding the facts of a question under discussion which, if disclosed, will show conclusively that right and reason are on your side. When this occurs, you should be prepared to argue on that basis.

It is true that I have expressed myself as opposed to objective research into the facts relating to the subject at issue, because I feel that such objective research can serve only to dampen your ardor and make your subsequent argument less forceful. However, in the final analysis I do not reject any effective means of argument, not even an appeal to truth and reason.

In this situation, however, a somewhat different technique is called for. Instead of trying to discredit your opponent or his argument by a play on words, the use of satire, an appeal to prejudice, or deliberately misconstruing his statements as you would normally do in trying to get the better of him, you should appeal to him to *join with you*, in looking into the facts. This is an appeal which he cannot gracefully refuse, particularly if you have not goaded him into an uncompromising stand on the subject by positive arguments of your own. The advantage of this technique is that it not only enables you to win the argument (without your opponent's realizing it, perhaps), but it might even result in his changing his own mind on the subject!

Conclusion

I do not claim to have presented a comprehensive exposition of the art of argument in this work. Indeed, examples of the described argumentative techniques which I have encountered over the years have been so numerous and so varied in their subtle nuances, that were I to try to include them all, I would never finish writing this book. Instead, I have given only a few basic examples of effective debating practices, with the hope that you will go on from there to find other effective arguments which you can use. I assume that my examples have already engendered other examples in your mind.

Take note of the effective arguments you encounter, write them down if necessary, adapt them to the issues of the day, try them out on your friends (if you still have any), note your arguments' effectiveness, and analyze them to find out why you have failed, if you have. In time, with diligent pursuance of this subject, the use of effective argumentative methods will become automatic and make you a debater to be reckoned with in any situation. The gentle art of argument will become an absorbing passion. I hope that it will prove to be as pleasant an avocation for you as it has been for me.

Good Luck!